My dear Rose,

As I fly into the darkness of space, I cast one last glance back
at the Planet of Coppelius. I can see both its sunlit side and
the side shrouded in shadow, and I remember the friends I
made on each side.

Coppelius tried to enrich his people by discovering a dazzling
new color, and to do so, he was willing to destroy the dark
half of his planet and the gentle beings who live there. In his
thirst for glory, he was blind to the recklessness of his plan
and deaf to the voice of anyone who disagreed with him.

Happily, he came to his senses and learned to recognize
the true beauty of both sunshine and shadow. I hope that in
the future, I shall encounter other leaders who are likewise
enlightened.

The Little Prince

First American edition published in 2015 by Graphic Universe™.

Le Petit Prince®

based on the masterpiece by Antoine de Saint-Exupéry

© 2015 LPPM
An animated series based on the novel *Le Petit Prince* by Antoine de Saint-Exupéry
Developed for television by Matthieu Delaporte, Alexandre de la Patellière, and Bertrand Gatignol
Directed by Pierre-Alain Chartier

© 2015 ÉDITIONS GLÉNAT
Copyright © 2015 by Lerner Publishing Group, Inc., for the current edition

Graphic Universe™ is a trademark of Lerner Publishing Group, Inc.

Graphic Universe™
A division of Lerner Publishing Group, Inc.
241 First Avenue North
Minneapolis, MN 55401 USA

For reading levels and more information, look up this title at www.lernerbooks.com.

Library of Congress Cataloging-in-Publication Data

Bruneau, Clotilde.
    [Planète des Okidiens. English]
    The planet of Okidians / story by Christel Gonnard and Thierry Gaudin ; design and illustrations by Nautilus Studio ; adaptation by Clotilde Bruneau ; translation: Anne Collins Smith and Owen Smith.—First American edition.
        pages   cm. — (The little prince ; #21)
    ISBN 978-0-7613-8771-8 (lib. bdg. : alk. paper) — ISBN 978-1-4677-6024-9 (pbk.) —
ISBN 978-1-4677-6196-3 (EB pdf)
    1. Graphic novels. I. Gonnard, Christel. II. Gaudin, Thierry. III. Smith, Anne Collins, translator.
IV. Smith, Owen (Owen M.), translator. V. Saint- Exupéry, Antoine de, 1900-1944. Petit Prince. VI. Nautilus Studio. VII. Petit Prince (Television program) VIII. Title.
PZ7.7.B8Pjf 2015
741.5'944—dc23   2014027562

Manufactured in the United States of America
1 — DP — 12/31/14

THE NEW ADVENTURES
BASED ON THE MASTERPIECE BY ANTOINE DE SAINT-EXUPÉRY

The Little Prince

THE PLANET OF OKIDIANS

Based on the animated series and an original story by Christel Gonnard and Thierry Gaudin

Design: Nautilus Studio
Story: Clotilde Bruneau
Artistic Direction: Didier Poli
Art: Diane Fayolle
Backgrounds: Jérôme Benoit
Coloring: Moonsun
Editing: Christine Chatal
Editorial Consultant: Didier Convard

Translation: Anne and Owen Smith

Graphic Universe™ • Minneapolis

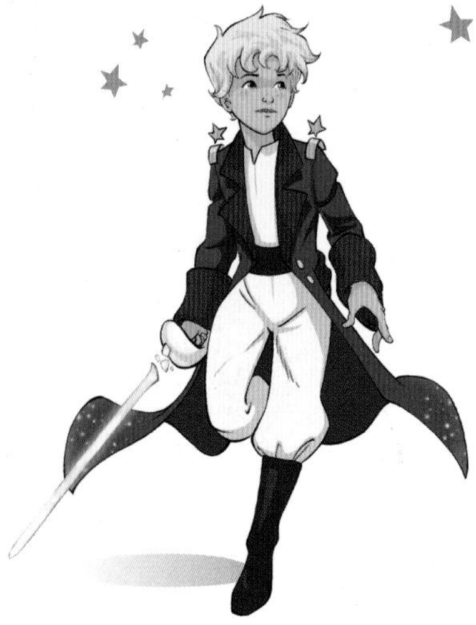

THE LITTLE PRINCE

The Little Prince has extraordinary gifts. His sense of wonder allows him to discover what no one else can see. The Little Prince can communicate with all the beings in the universe, even the animals and plants. His powers grow over the course of his adventures.

The Prince's uniform:
When he transforms into the uniform of a prince, he is more agile and quick. When faced with difficult situations, the Little Prince also uses a sword that lets him sketch and bring to life anything from his imagination.

His sketchbook:
When he is not in his Prince's clothing, the Little Prince carries a sketchbook. When he blows on the pages, they take wing and form objects that he'll find very useful. Like his sword, it's powered by stardust collected on his travels.

FOX

A grouch, a trickster, and, so he says, interested only in his next meal, Fox is in reality the Little Prince's best friend. As such, he is always there to give him help but also just as much to help him to grow and to learn about the world.

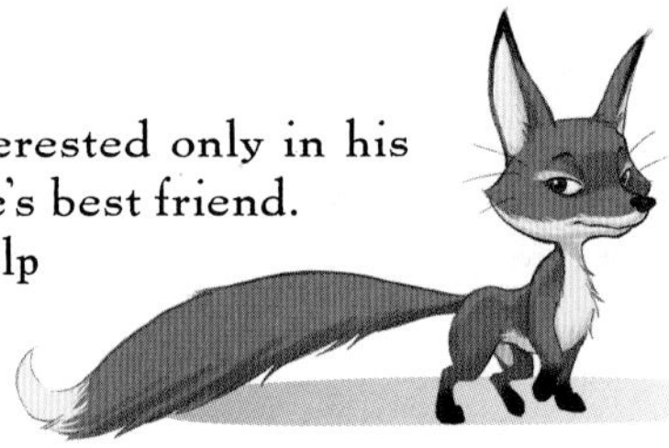

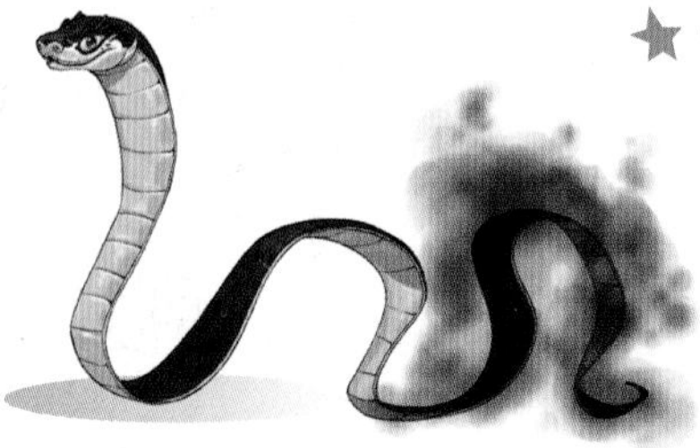

THE SNAKE

Even though the Little Prince still does not know exactly why, there can be no doubt that the Snake has set his mind to plunging the entire universe into darkness! And to accomplish his goal, this malicious being is ready to use any form of deception. However, the Snake never takes action himself. He prefers to bring out the wickedness in those beings he has chosen to bite, tempting them to put their own worlds in danger.

THE GLOOMIES

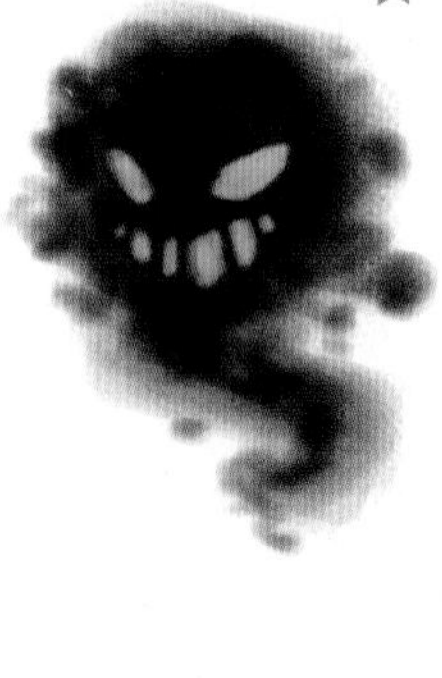

When people who have been "bitten" by the Snake have completely destroyed their own planets, they become Gloomies, slaves to their Snake master. The Gloomies act as a group and carry out the Snake's most vile orders so he can get the better of the Little Prince!

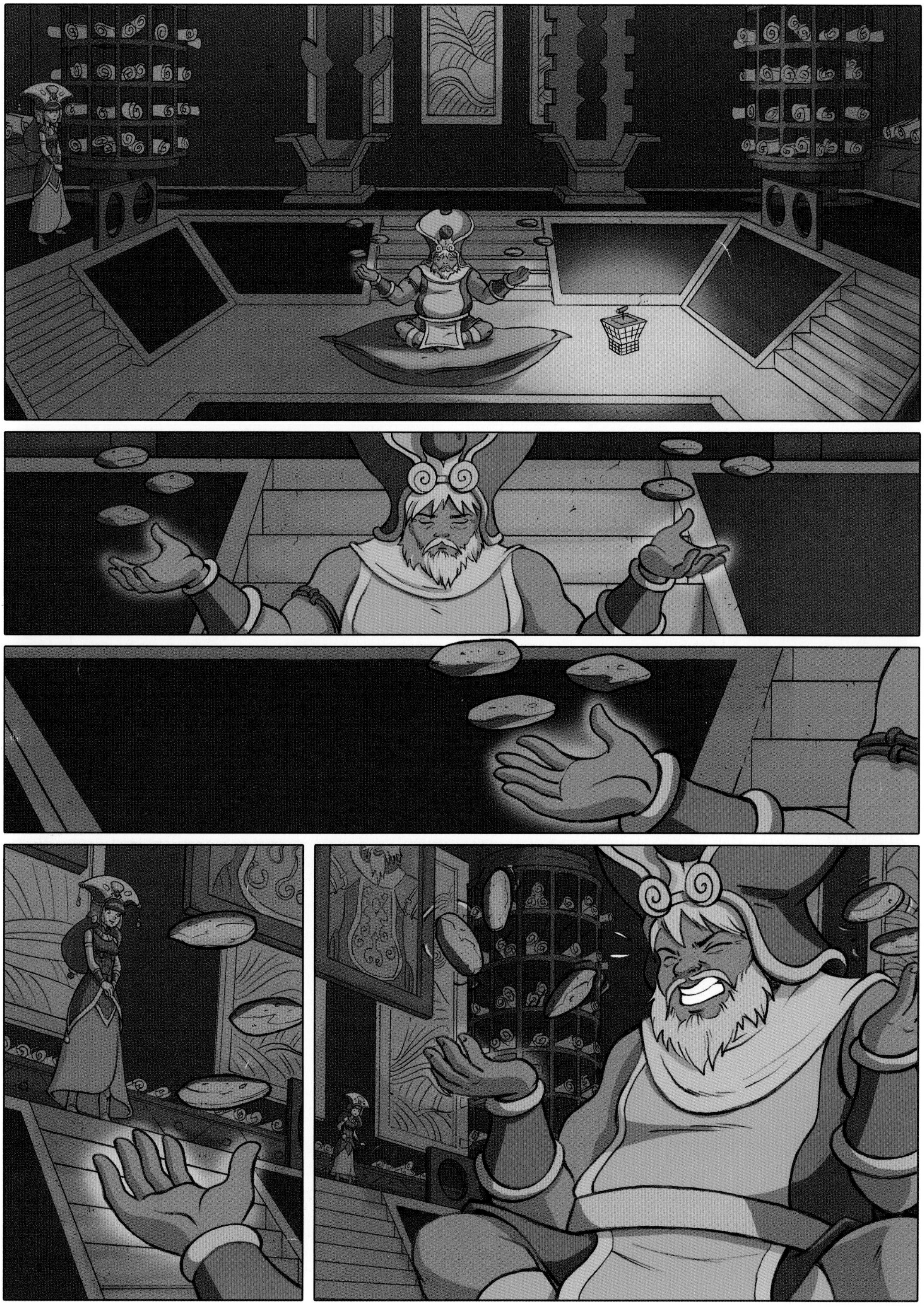

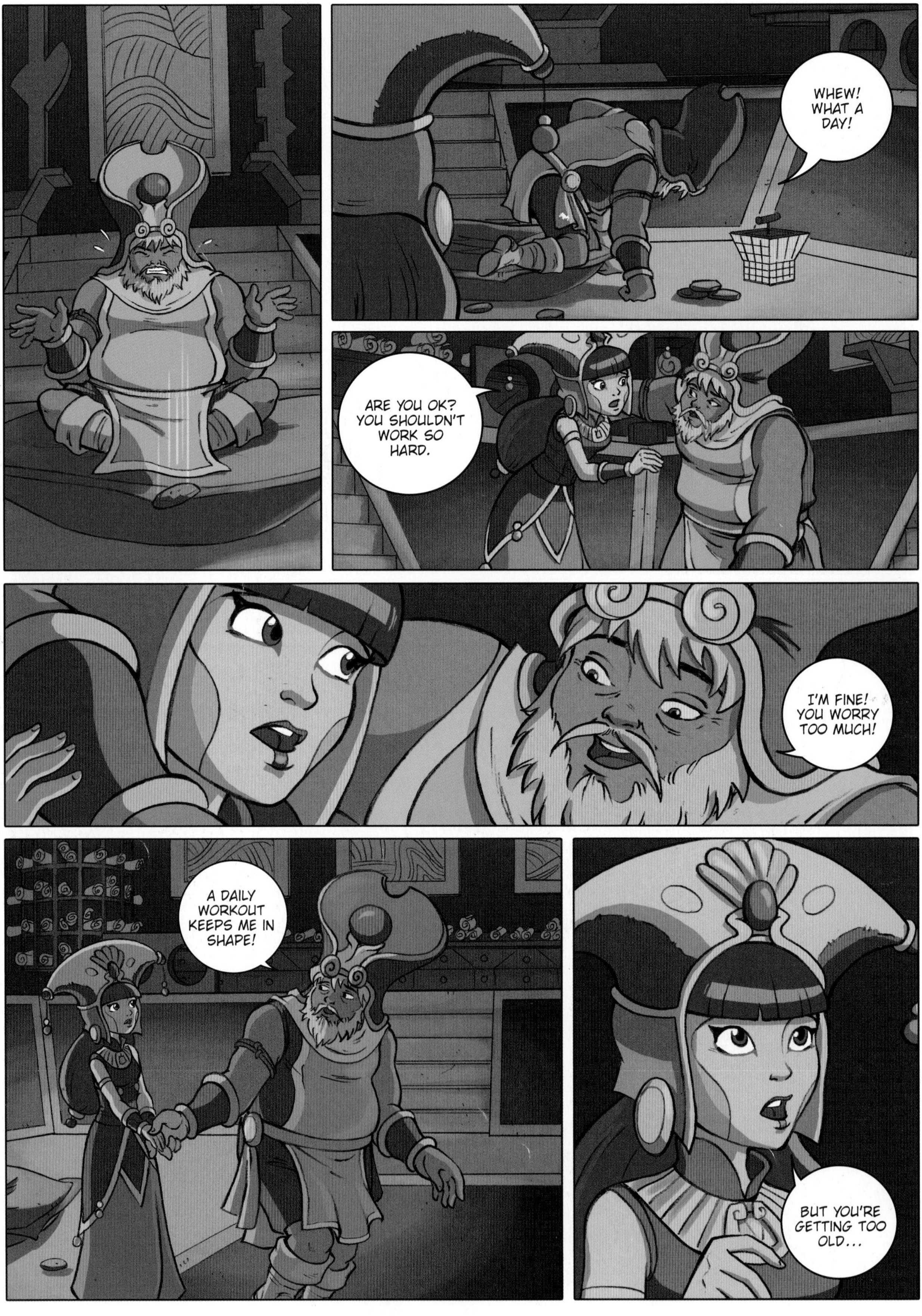
WHEW! WHAT A DAY!
ARE YOU OK? YOU SHOULDN'T WORK SO HARD.
I'M FINE! YOU WORRY TOO MUCH!
A DAILY WORKOUT KEEPS ME IN SHAPE!
BUT YOU'RE GETTING TOO OLD...

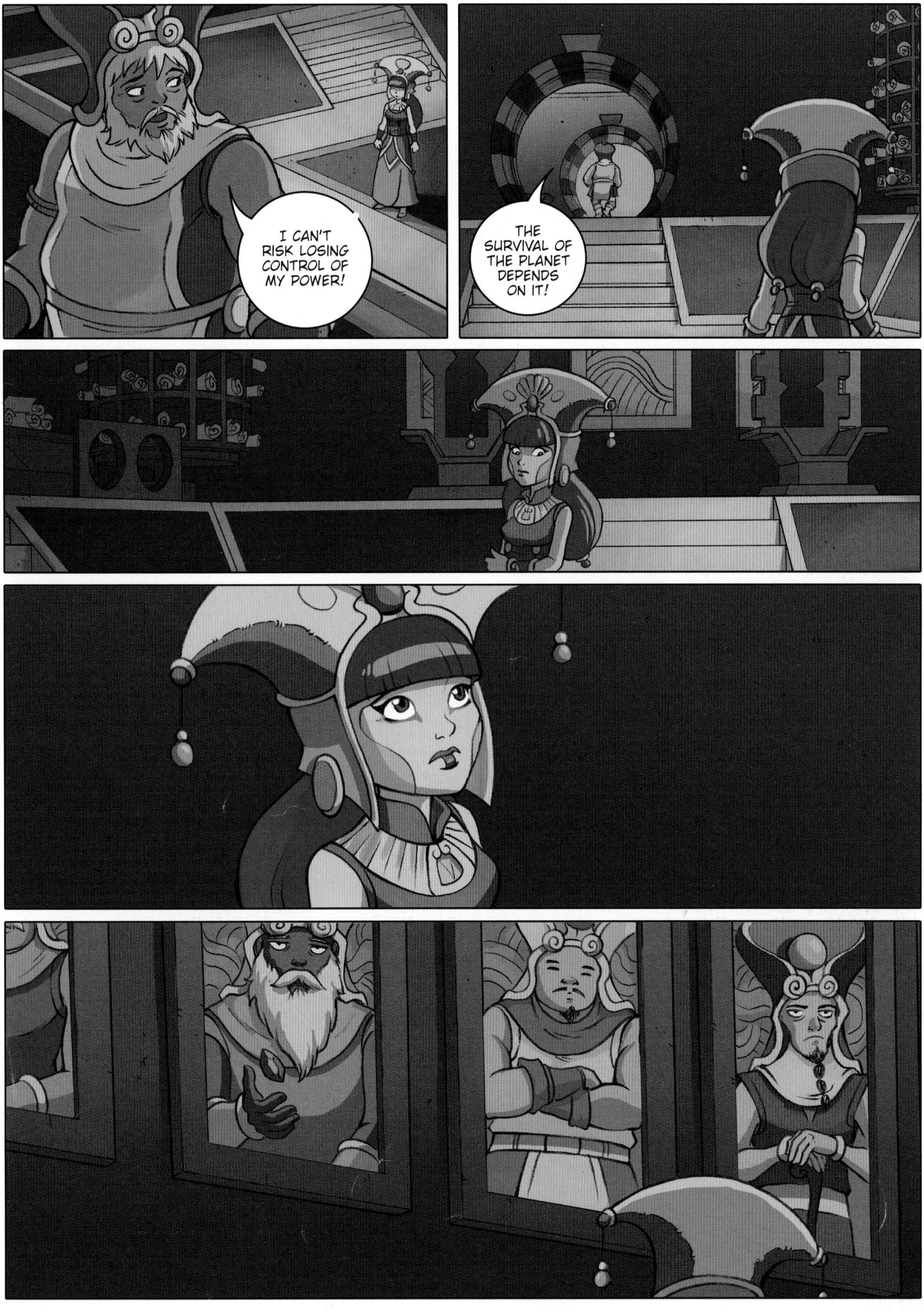
I CAN'T RISK LOSING CONTROL OF MY POWER!
THE SURVIVAL OF THE PLANET DEPENDS ON IT!

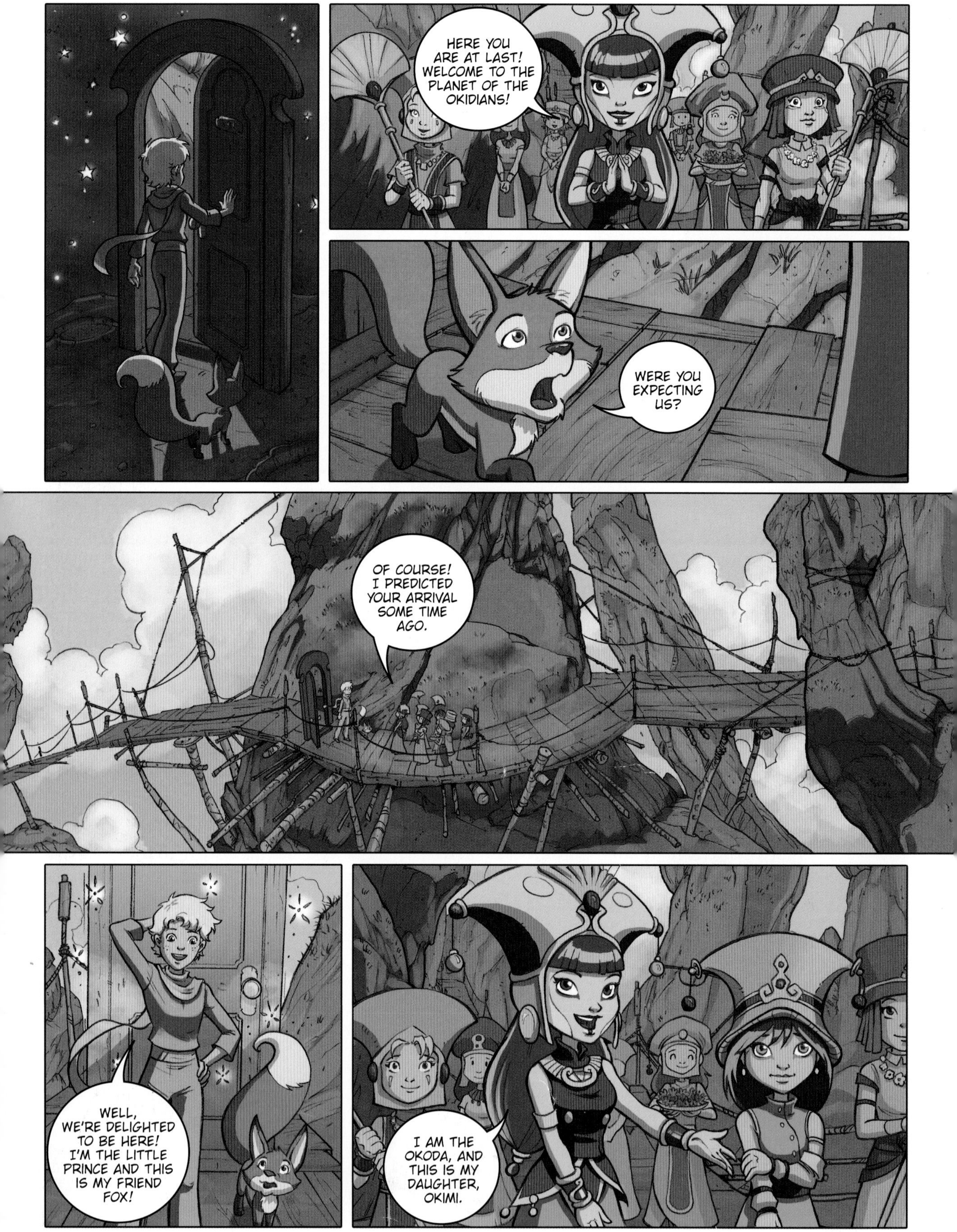
HERE YOU ARE AT LAST! WELCOME TO THE PLANET OF THE OKIDIANS!
WERE YOU EXPECTING US?
OF COURSE! I PREDICTED YOUR ARRIVAL SOME TIME AGO.
WELL, WE'RE DELIGHTED TO BE HERE! I'M THE LITTLE PRINCE AND THIS IS MY FRIEND FOX!
I AM THE OKODA, AND THIS IS MY DAUGHTER, OKIMI.

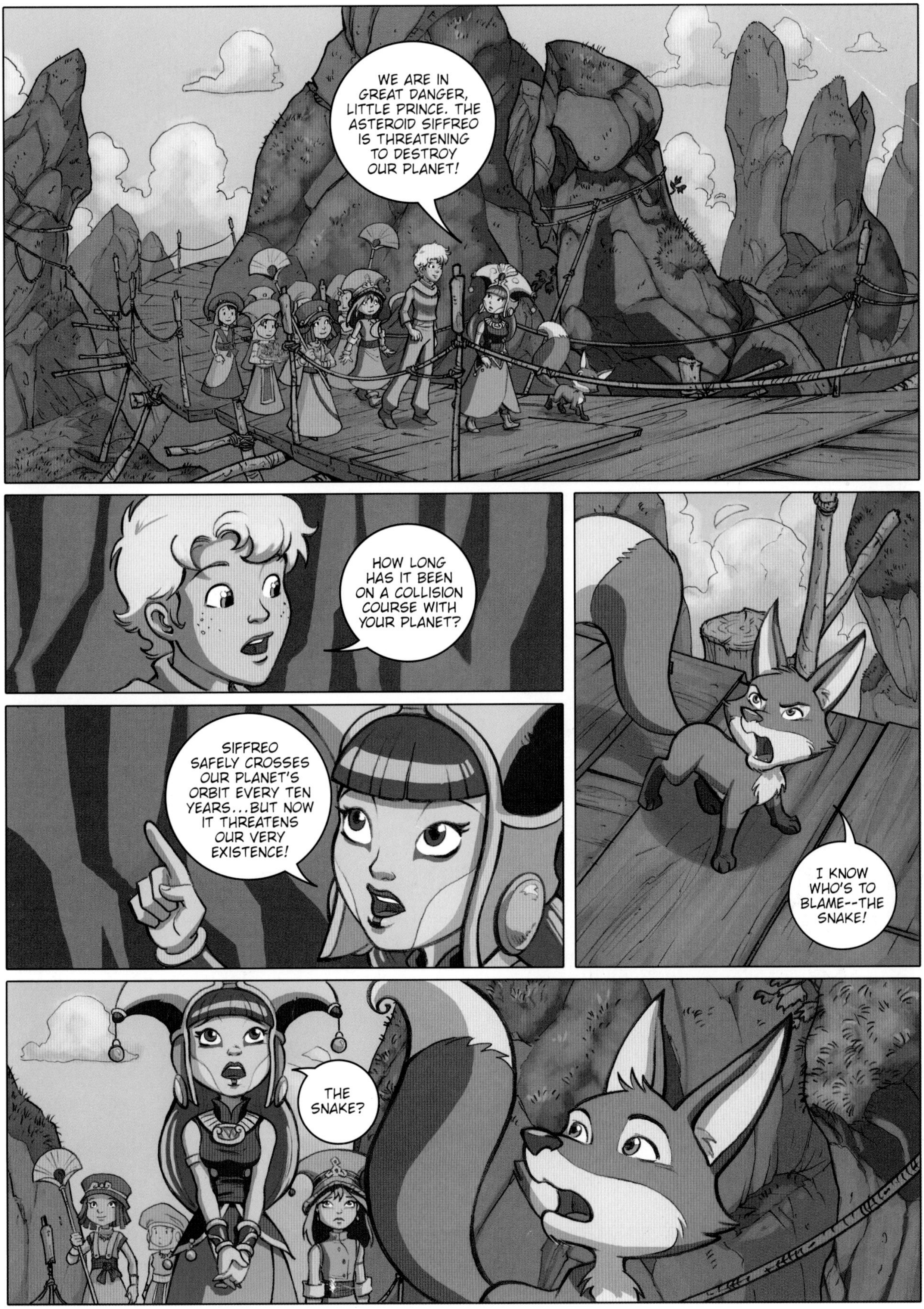
WE ARE IN GREAT DANGER, LITTLE PRINCE. THE ASTEROID SIFFREO IS THREATENING TO DESTROY OUR PLANET!
HOW LONG HAS IT BEEN ON A COLLISION COURSE WITH YOUR PLANET?
SIFFREO SAFELY CROSSES OUR PLANET'S ORBIT EVERY TEN YEARS...BUT NOW IT THREATENS OUR VERY EXISTENCE!
I KNOW WHO'S TO BLAME--THE SNAKE!
THE SNAKE?

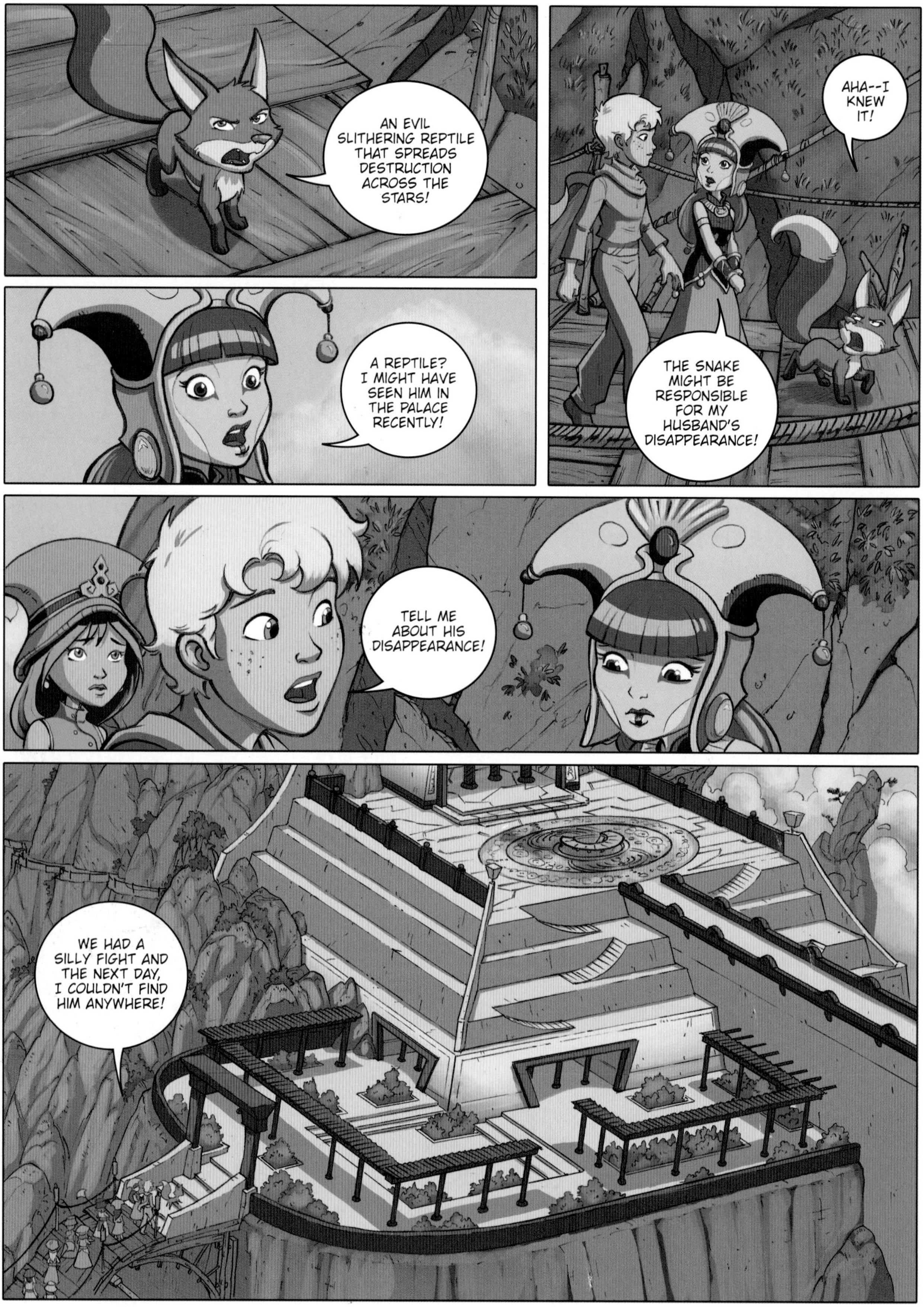
AN EVIL SLITHERING REPTILE THAT SPREADS DESTRUCTION ACROSS THE STARS!
AHA--I KNEW IT!
A REPTILE? I MIGHT HAVE SEEN HIM IN THE PALACE RECENTLY!
THE SNAKE MIGHT BE RESPONSIBLE FOR MY HUSBAND'S DISAPPEARANCE!
TELL ME ABOUT HIS DISAPPEARANCE!
WE HAD A SILLY FIGHT AND THE NEXT DAY, I COULDN'T FIND HIM ANYWHERE!

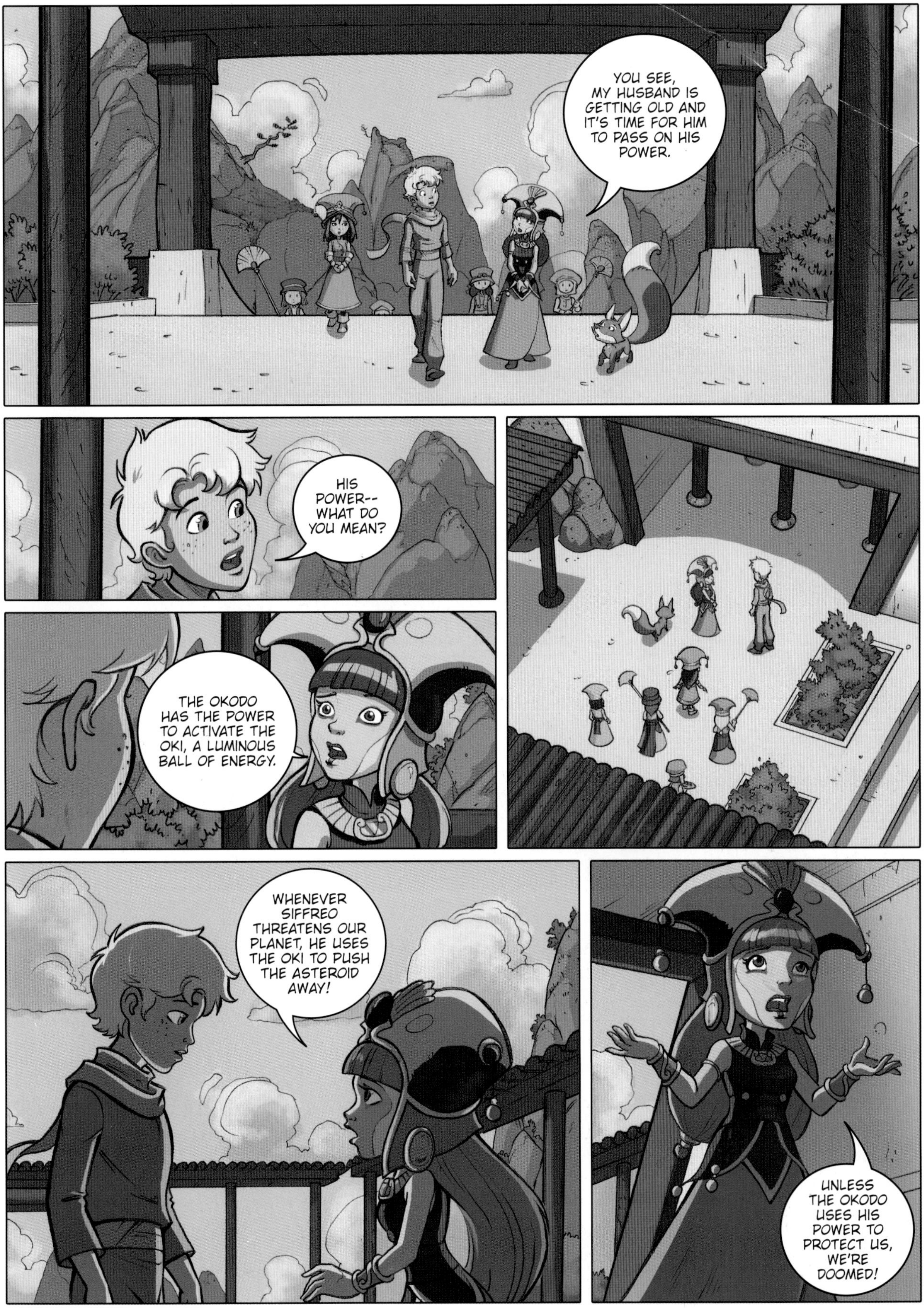
YOU SEE, MY HUSBAND IS GETTING OLD AND IT'S TIME FOR HIM TO PASS ON HIS POWER.
HIS POWER-- WHAT DO YOU MEAN?
THE OKODO HAS THE POWER TO ACTIVATE THE OKI, A LUMINOUS BALL OF ENERGY.
WHENEVER SIFFREO THREATENS OUR PLANET, HE USES THE OKI TO PUSH THE ASTEROID AWAY!
UNLESS THE OKODO USES HIS POWER TO PROTECT US, WE'RE DOOMED!

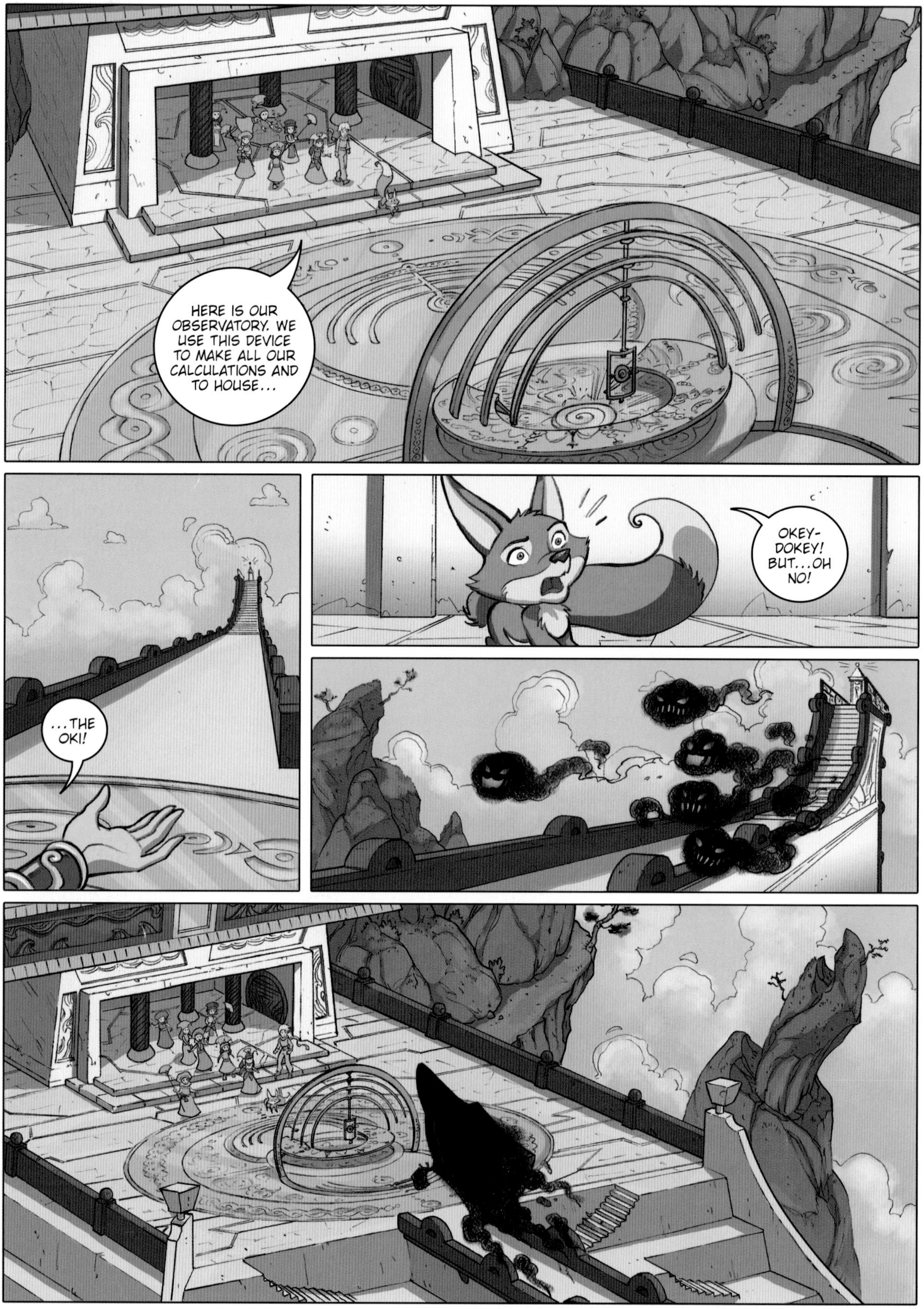
HERE IS OUR OBSERVATORY. WE USE THIS DEVICE TO MAKE ALL OUR CALCULATIONS AND TO HOUSE...
...THE OKI!
OKEY-DOKEY! BUT...OH NO!

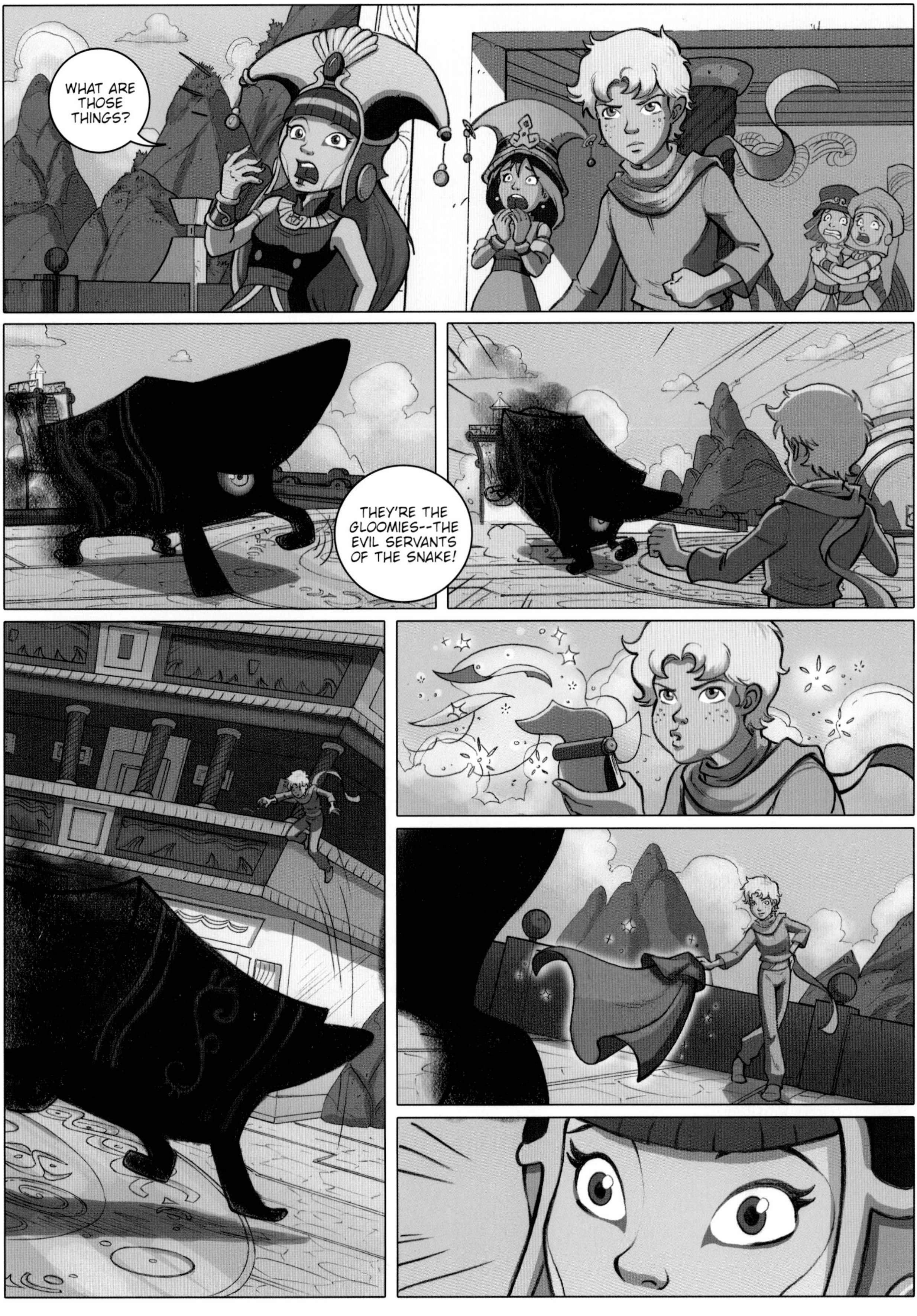
WHAT ARE THOSE THINGS?
THEY'RE THE GLOOMIES--THE EVIL SERVANTS OF THE SNAKE!

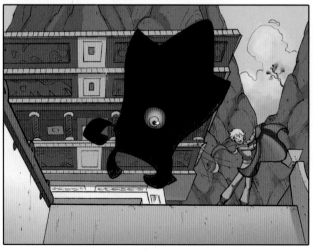

I'M
SURPRISED
IT WAS SO
EASY!

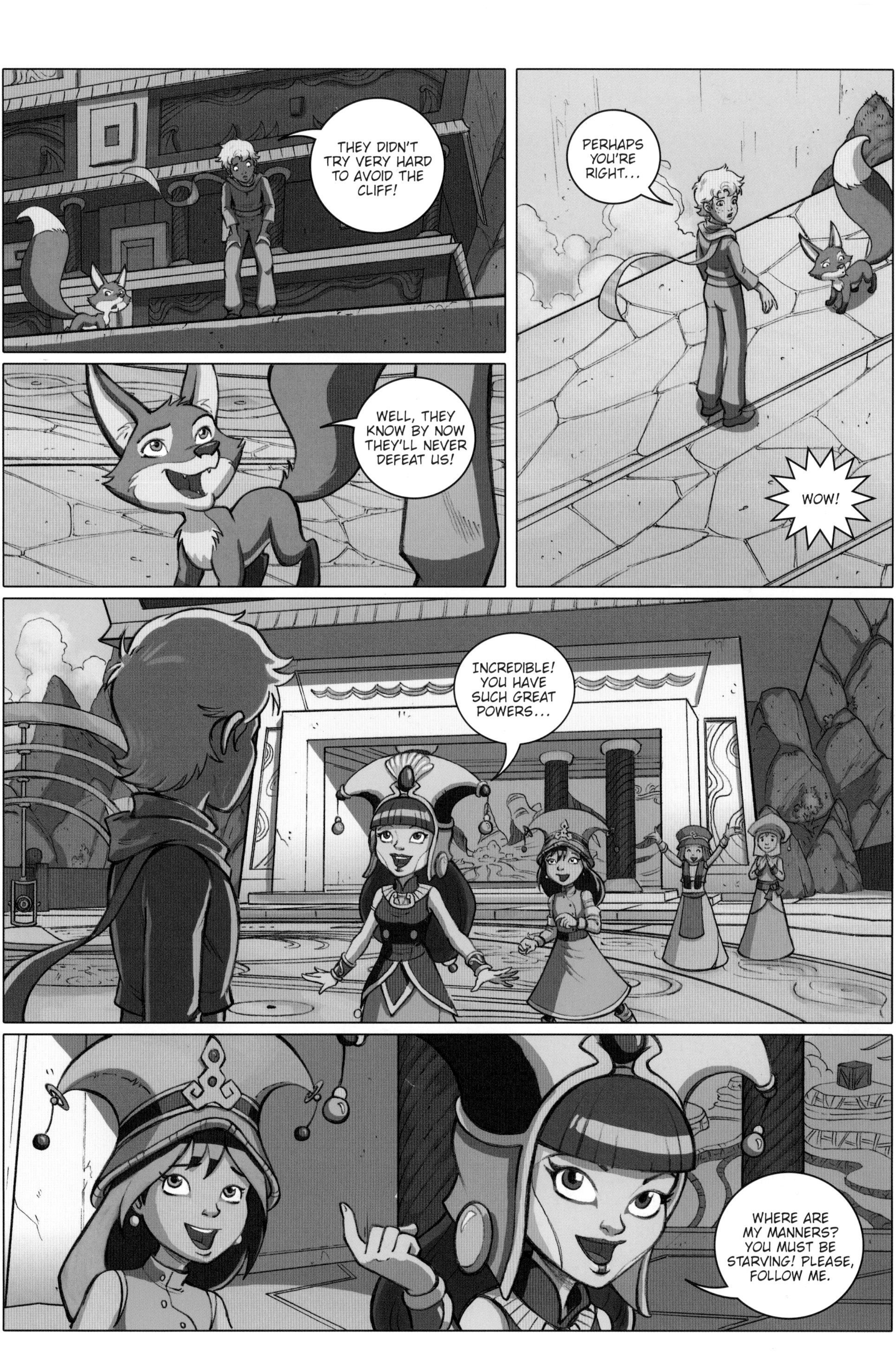

THEY DIDN'T TRY VERY HARD TO AVOID THE CLIFF!
PERHAPS YOU'RE RIGHT...
WELL, THEY KNOW BY NOW THEY'LL NEVER DEFEAT US!
WOW!
INCREDIBLE! YOU HAVE SUCH GREAT POWERS...
WHERE ARE MY MANNERS? YOU MUST BE STARVING! PLEASE, FOLLOW ME.

WHAT A CIVILIZED PLANET!

OKIMI, WHERE HAVE ALL THE MEN GONE?

THEY SET OUT ON AN EXPEDITION TO FIND THE OKODO... AND DISAPPEARED! NOW ONLY THE WOMEN ARE LEFT TO SAVE THE PLANET.

MOM, I REALLY THINK...

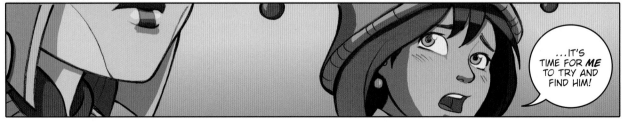

...IT'S TIME FOR *ME* TO TRY AND FIND HIM!

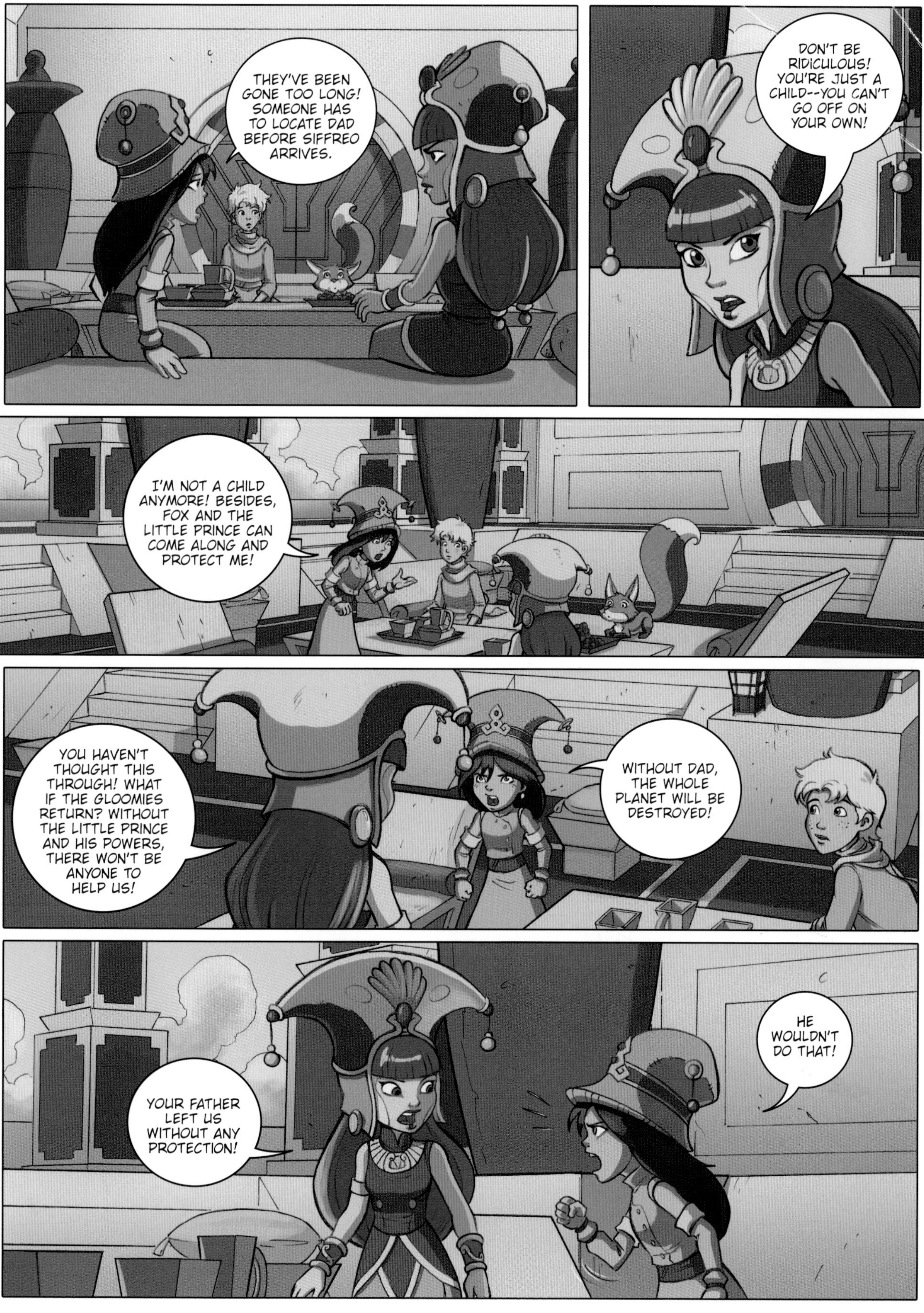
THEY'VE BEEN GONE TOO LONG! SOMEONE HAS TO LOCATE DAD BEFORE SIFFREO ARRIVES.
DON'T BE RIDICULOUS! YOU'RE JUST A CHILD--YOU CAN'T GO OFF ON YOUR OWN!
I'M NOT A CHILD ANYMORE! BESIDES, FOX AND THE LITTLE PRINCE CAN COME ALONG AND PROTECT ME!
YOU HAVEN'T THOUGHT THIS THROUGH! WHAT IF THE GLOOMIES RETURN? WITHOUT THE LITTLE PRINCE AND HIS POWERS, THERE WON'T BE ANYONE TO HELP US!
WITHOUT DAD, THE WHOLE PLANET WILL BE DESTROYED!
YOUR FATHER LEFT US WITHOUT ANY PROTECTION!
HE WOULDN'T DO THAT!

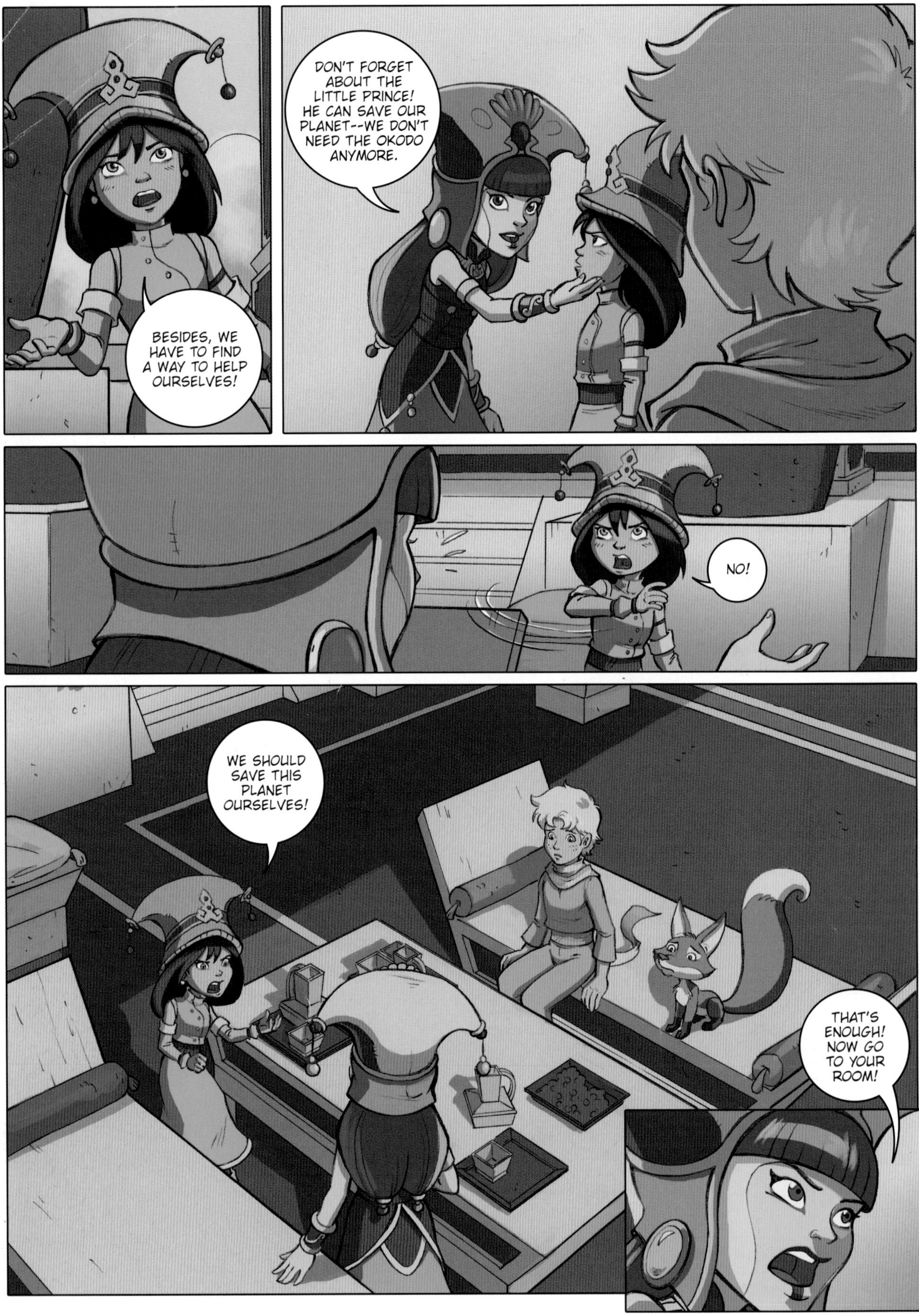
DON'T FORGET ABOUT THE LITTLE PRINCE! HE CAN SAVE OUR PLANET--WE DON'T NEED THE OKODO ANYMORE.
BESIDES, WE HAVE TO FIND A WAY TO HELP OURSELVES!
NO!
WE SHOULD SAVE THIS PLANET OURSELVES!
THAT'S ENOUGH! NOW GO TO YOUR ROOM!

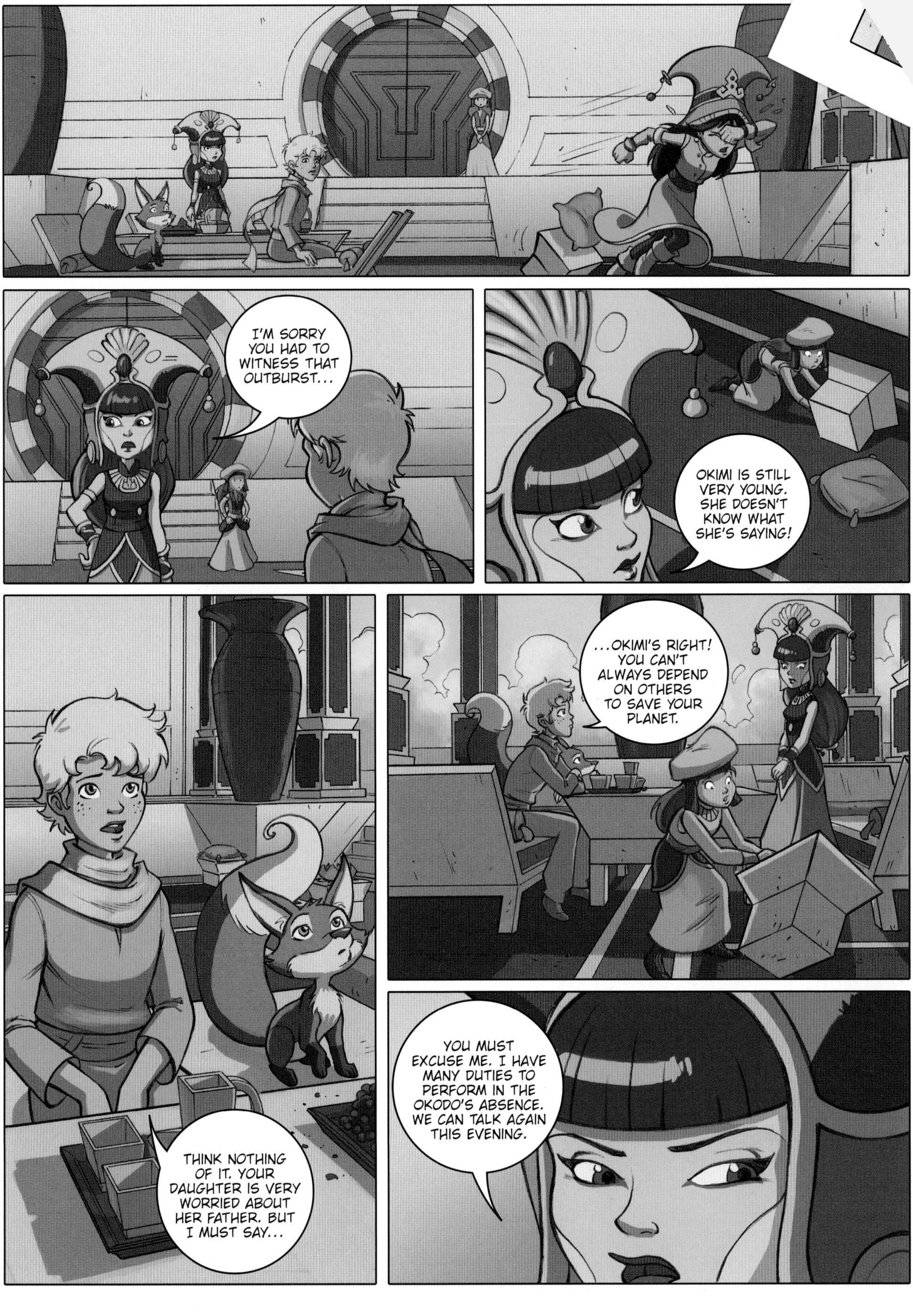
I'M SORRY YOU HAD TO WITNESS THAT OUTBURST...
OKIMI IS STILL VERY YOUNG. SHE DOESN'T KNOW WHAT SHE'S SAYING!
THINK NOTHING OF IT. YOUR DAUGHTER IS VERY WORRIED ABOUT HER FATHER. BUT I MUST SAY...
...OKIMI'S RIGHT! YOU CAN'T ALWAYS DEPEND ON OTHERS TO SAVE YOUR PLANET.
YOU MUST EXCUSE ME. I HAVE MANY DUTIES TO PERFORM IN THE OKODO'S ABSENCE. WE CAN TALK AGAIN THIS EVENING.

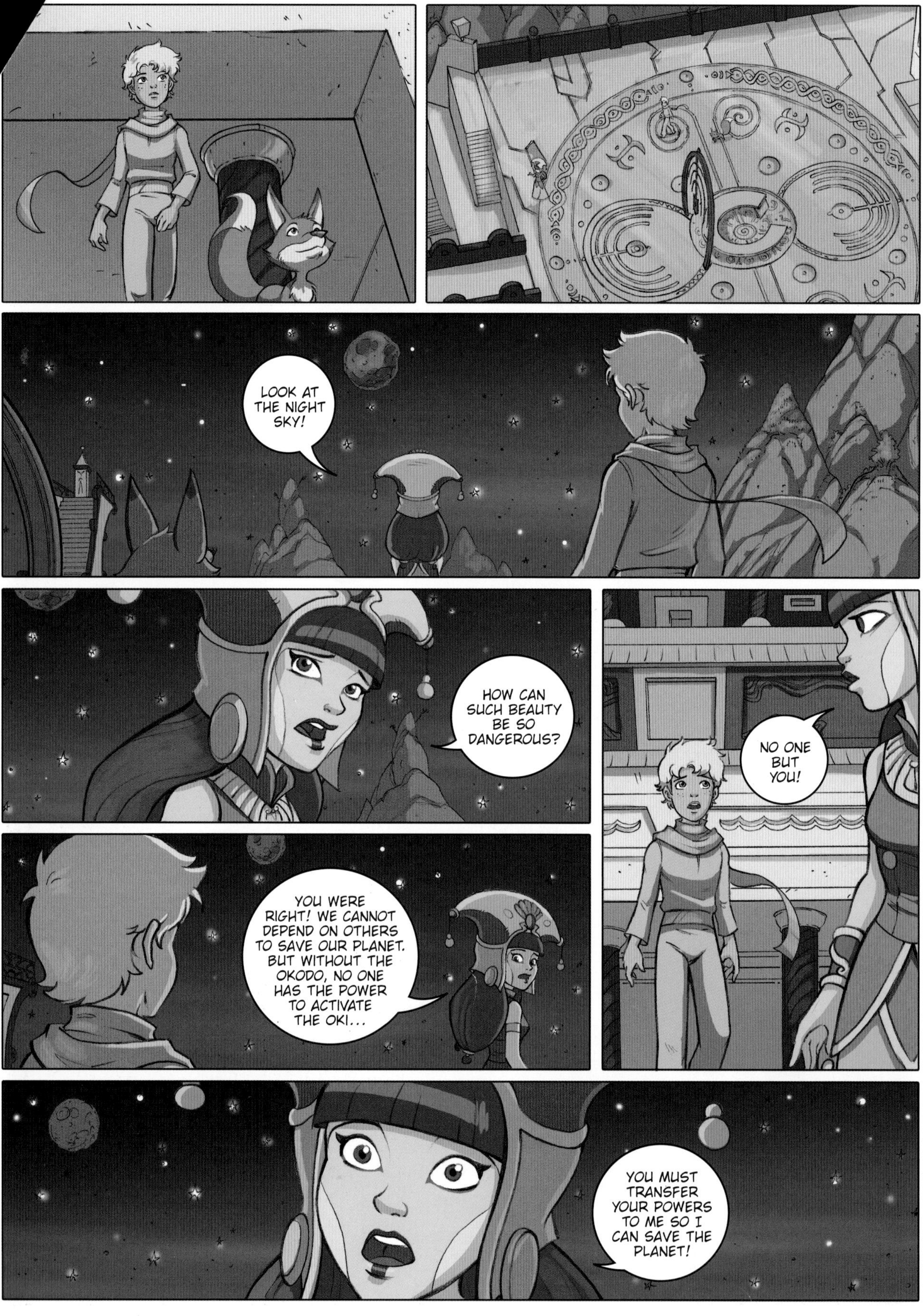
LOOK AT THE NIGHT SKY!
HOW CAN SUCH BEAUTY BE SO DANGEROUS?
YOU WERE RIGHT! WE CANNOT DEPEND ON OTHERS TO SAVE OUR PLANET. BUT WITHOUT THE OKODO, NO ONE HAS THE POWER TO ACTIVATE THE OKI...
NO ONE BUT YOU!
YOU MUST TRANSFER YOUR POWERS TO ME SO I CAN SAVE THE PLANET!

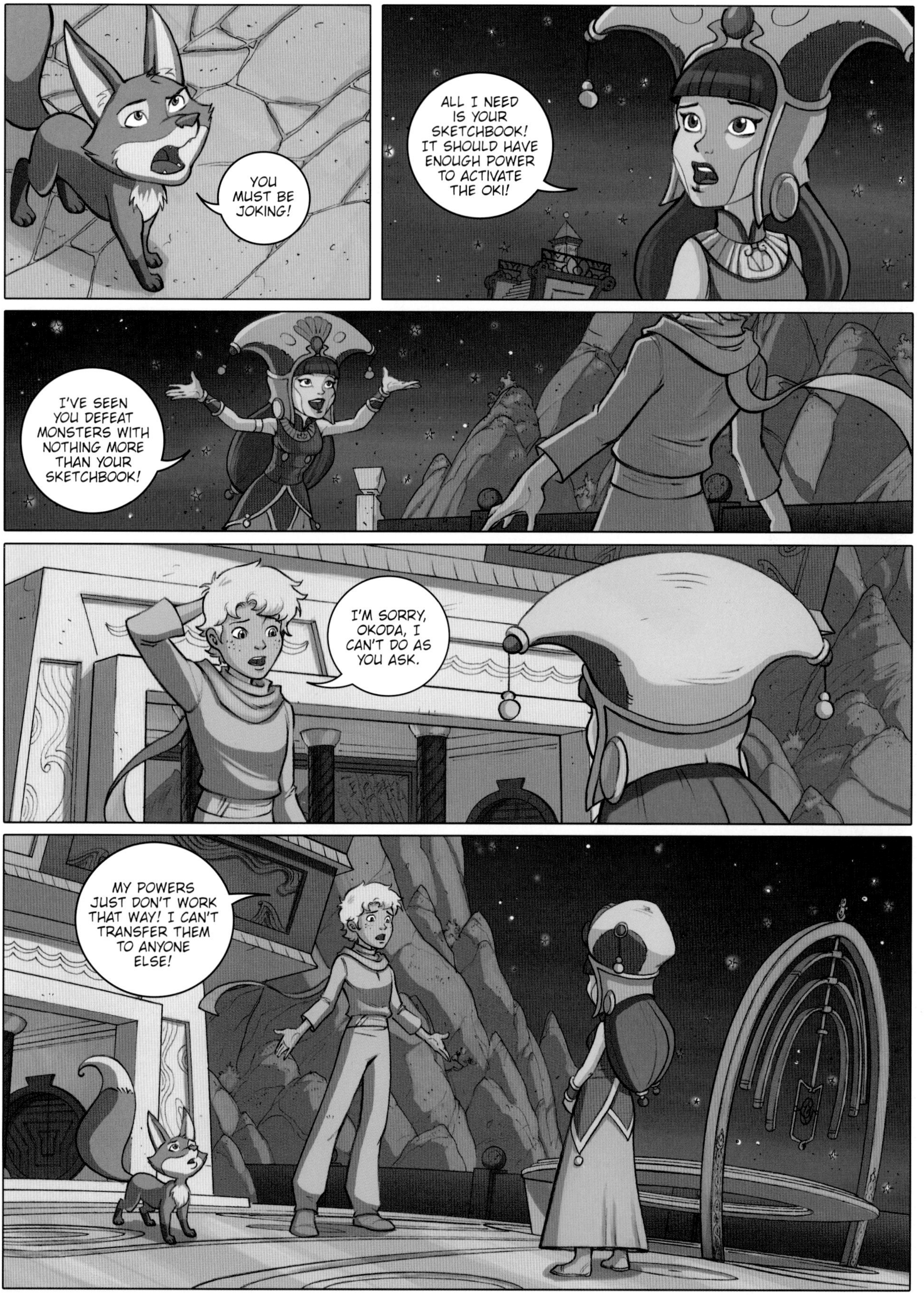
YOU MUST BE JOKING!
ALL I NEED IS YOUR SKETCHBOOK! IT SHOULD HAVE ENOUGH POWER TO ACTIVATE THE OKI!
I'VE SEEN YOU DEFEAT MONSTERS WITH NOTHING MORE THAN YOUR SKETCHBOOK!
I'M SORRY, OKODA, I CAN'T DO AS YOU ASK.
MY POWERS JUST DON'T WORK THAT WAY! I CAN'T TRANSFER THEM TO ANYONE ELSE!

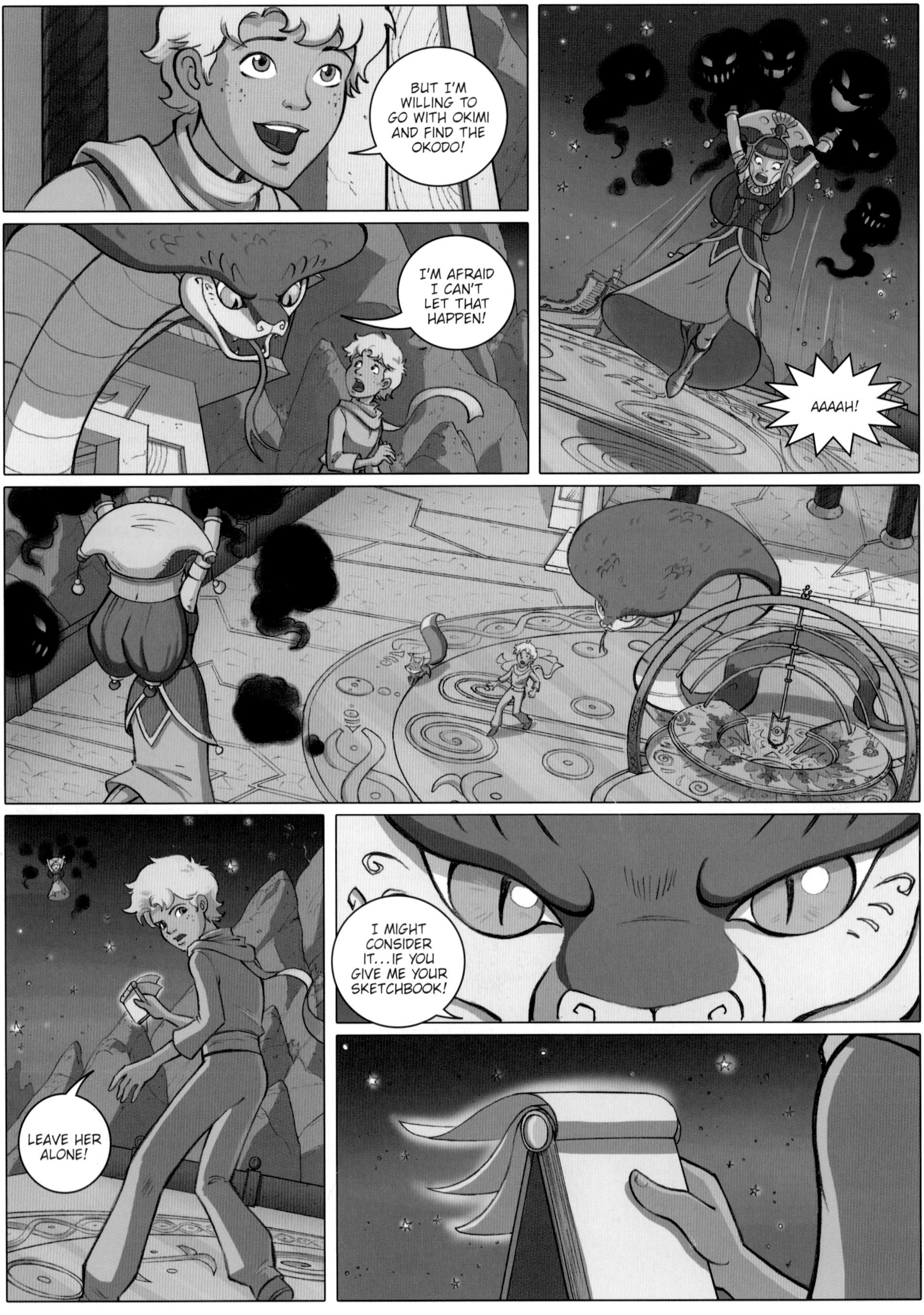
BUT I'M WILLING TO GO WITH OKIMI AND FIND THE OKODO!
AAAAH!
I'M AFRAID I CAN'T LET THAT HAPPEN!
LEAVE HER ALONE!
I MIGHT CONSIDER IT...IF YOU GIVE ME YOUR SKETCHBOOK!

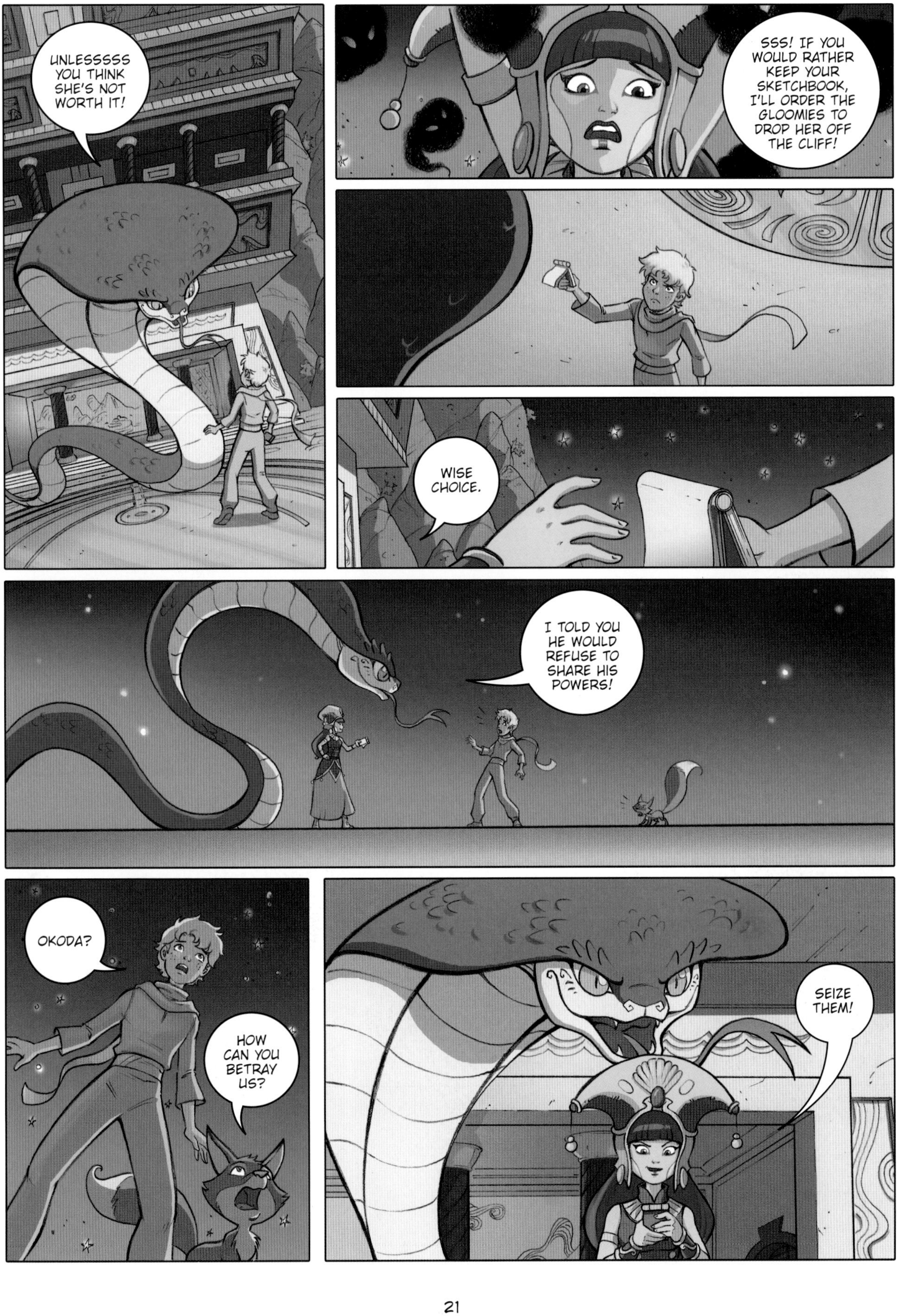
UNLESSSSS YOU THINK SHE'S NOT WORTH IT!
SSS! IF YOU WOULD RATHER KEEP YOUR SKETCHBOOK, I'LL ORDER THE GLOOMIES TO DROP HER OFF THE CLIFF!
WISE CHOICE.
I TOLD YOU HE WOULD REFUSE TO SHARE HIS POWERS!
OKODA?
HOW CAN YOU BETRAY US?
SEIZE THEM!

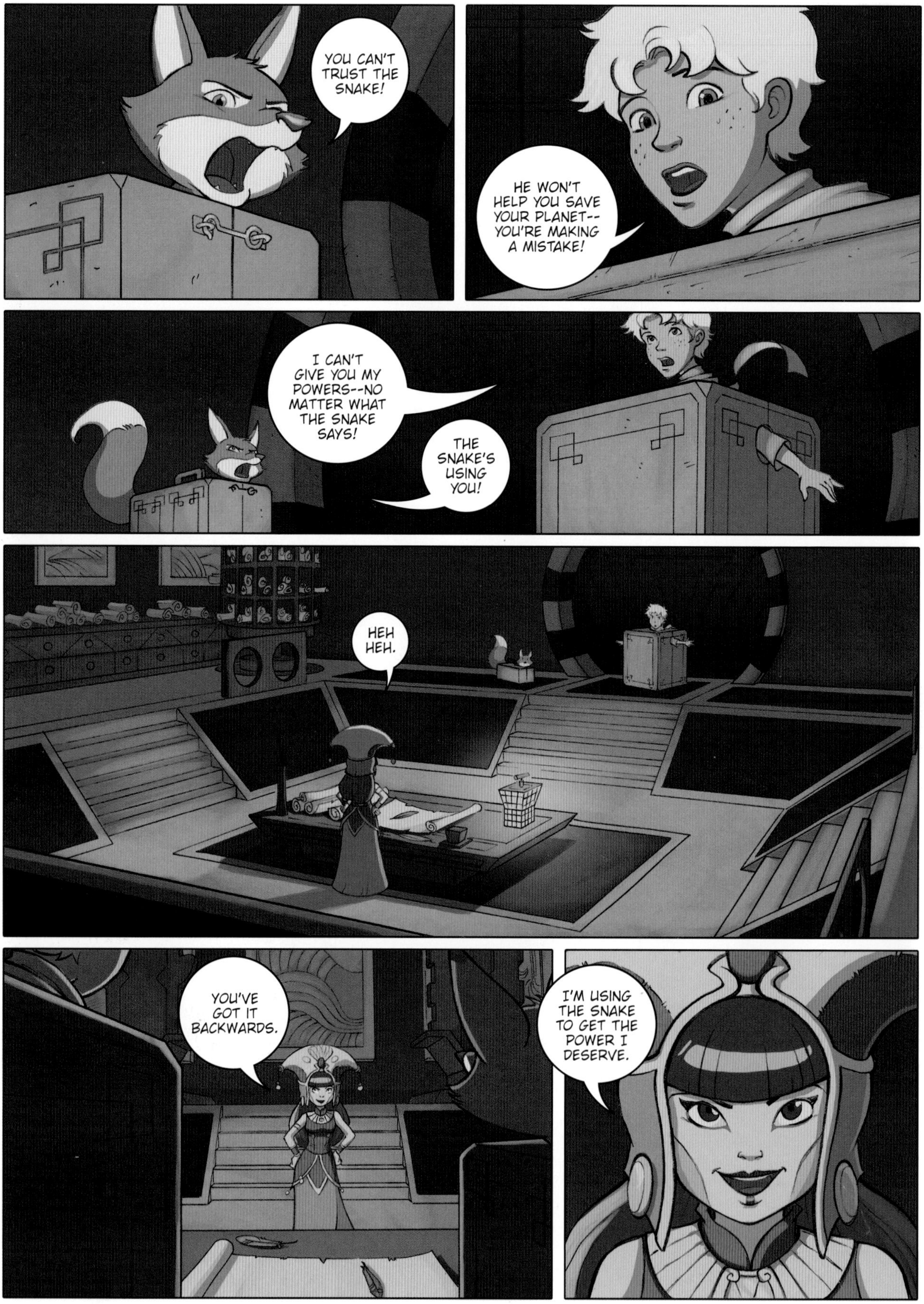
YOU CAN'T TRUST THE SNAKE!
HE WON'T HELP YOU SAVE YOUR PLANET-- YOU'RE MAKING A MISTAKE!
I CAN'T GIVE YOU MY POWERS--NO MATTER WHAT THE SNAKE SAYS!
THE SNAKE'S USING YOU!
HEH HEH.
YOU'VE GOT IT BACKWARDS.
I'M USING THE SNAKE TO GET THE POWER I DESERVE.

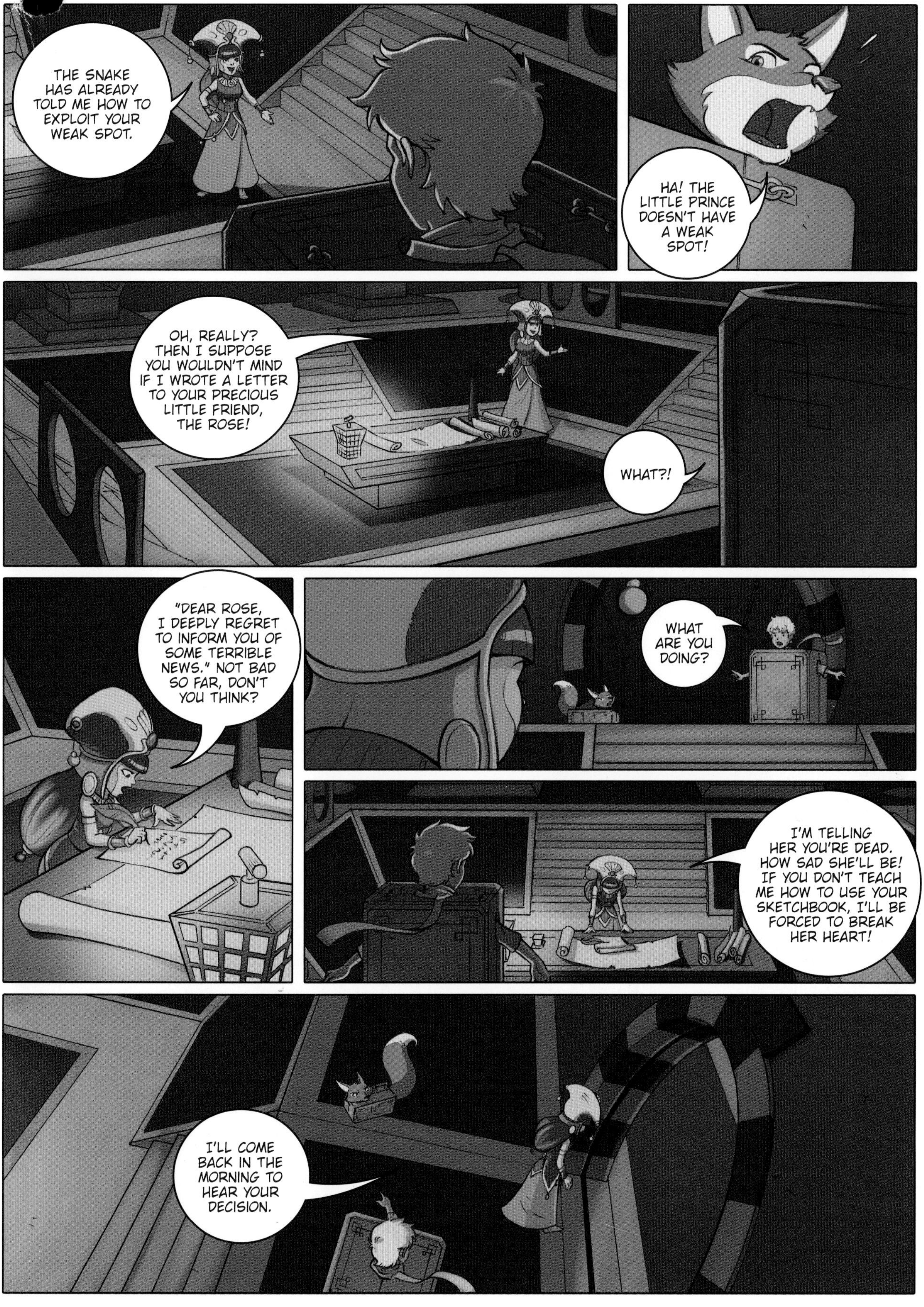
THE SNAKE HAS ALREADY TOLD ME HOW TO EXPLOIT YOUR WEAK SPOT.
HA! THE LITTLE PRINCE DOESN'T HAVE A WEAK SPOT!
OH, REALLY? THEN I SUPPOSE YOU WOULDN'T MIND IF I WROTE A LETTER TO YOUR PRECIOUS LITTLE FRIEND, THE ROSE!
WHAT?!
"DEAR ROSE, I DEEPLY REGRET TO INFORM YOU OF SOME TERRIBLE NEWS." NOT BAD SO FAR, DON'T YOU THINK?
WHAT ARE YOU DOING?
I'M TELLING HER YOU'RE DEAD. HOW SAD SHE'LL BE! IF YOU DON'T TEACH ME HOW TO USE YOUR SKETCHBOOK, I'LL BE FORCED TO BREAK HER HEART!
I'LL COME BACK IN THE MORNING TO HEAR YOUR DECISION.

PSSST!

I WAS TRYING TO FIND CLUES ABOUT MY FATHER'S DISAPPEARANCE WHEN I HEARD MY MOTHER'S VOICE...

OKIMI!

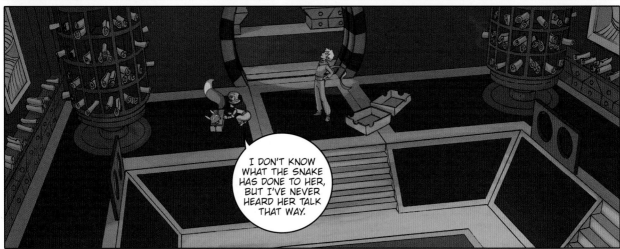

I DON'T KNOW WHAT THE SNAKE HAS DONE TO HER, BUT I'VE NEVER HEARD HER TALK THAT WAY.

THANKS, OKIMI!

I KNOW A WAY YOU CAN PAY ME BACK!

HELP ME FIND MY FATHER!

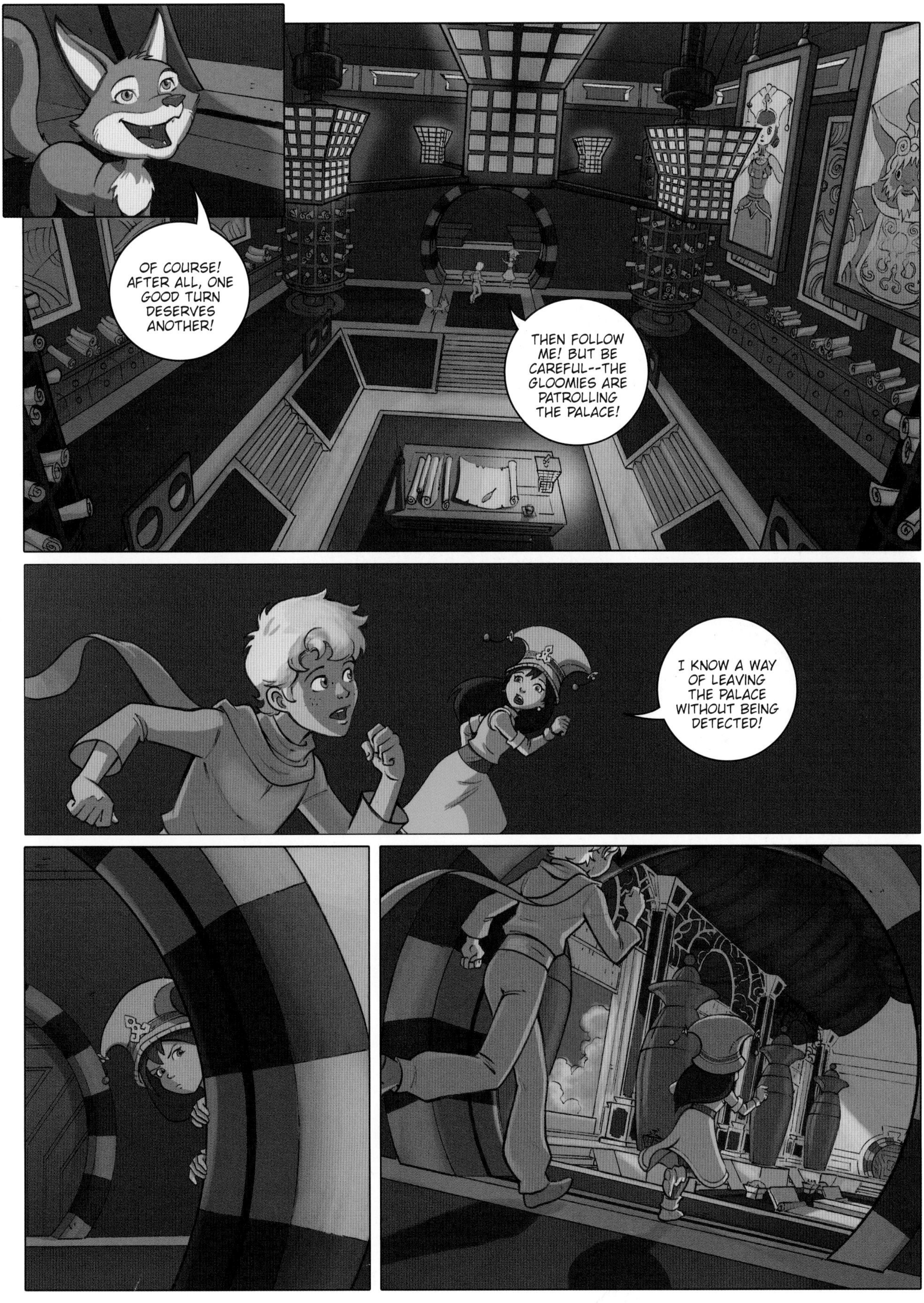
OF COURSE! AFTER ALL, ONE GOOD TURN DESERVES ANOTHER!
THEN FOLLOW ME! BUT BE CAREFUL--THE GLOOMIES ARE PATROLLING THE PALACE!
I KNOW A WAY OF LEAVING THE PALACE WITHOUT BEING DETECTED!

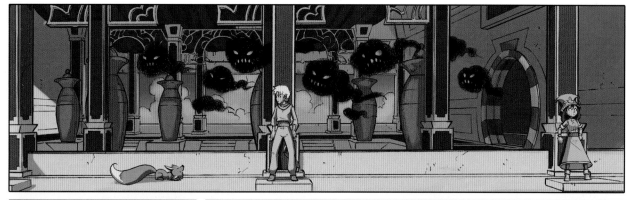

THEY'VE SPOTTED US!

THAT WAS CLOSE!

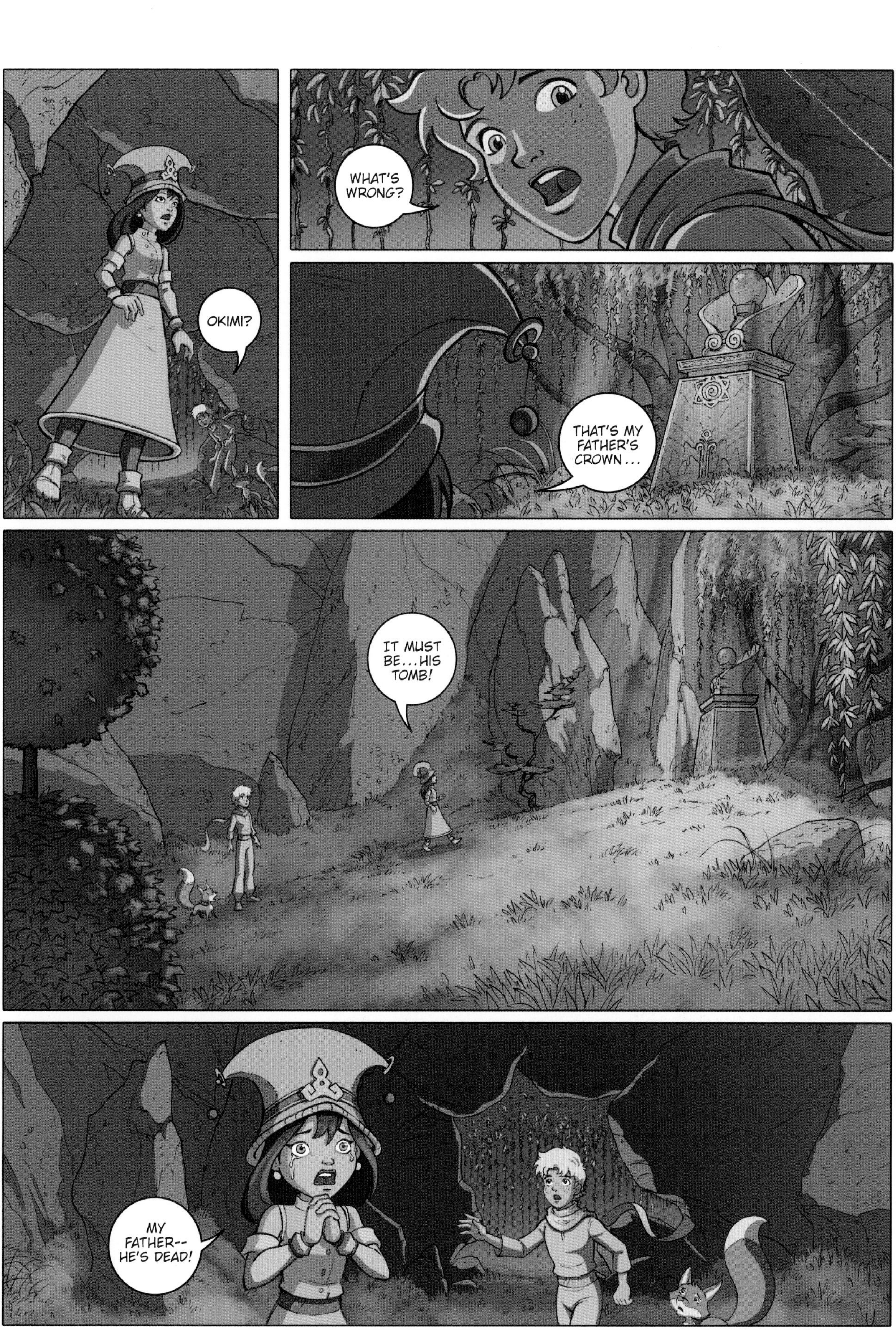
OKIMI?
WHAT'S WRONG?
THAT'S MY FATHER'S CROWN...
IT MUST BE...HIS TOMB!
MY FATHER-- HE'S DEAD!

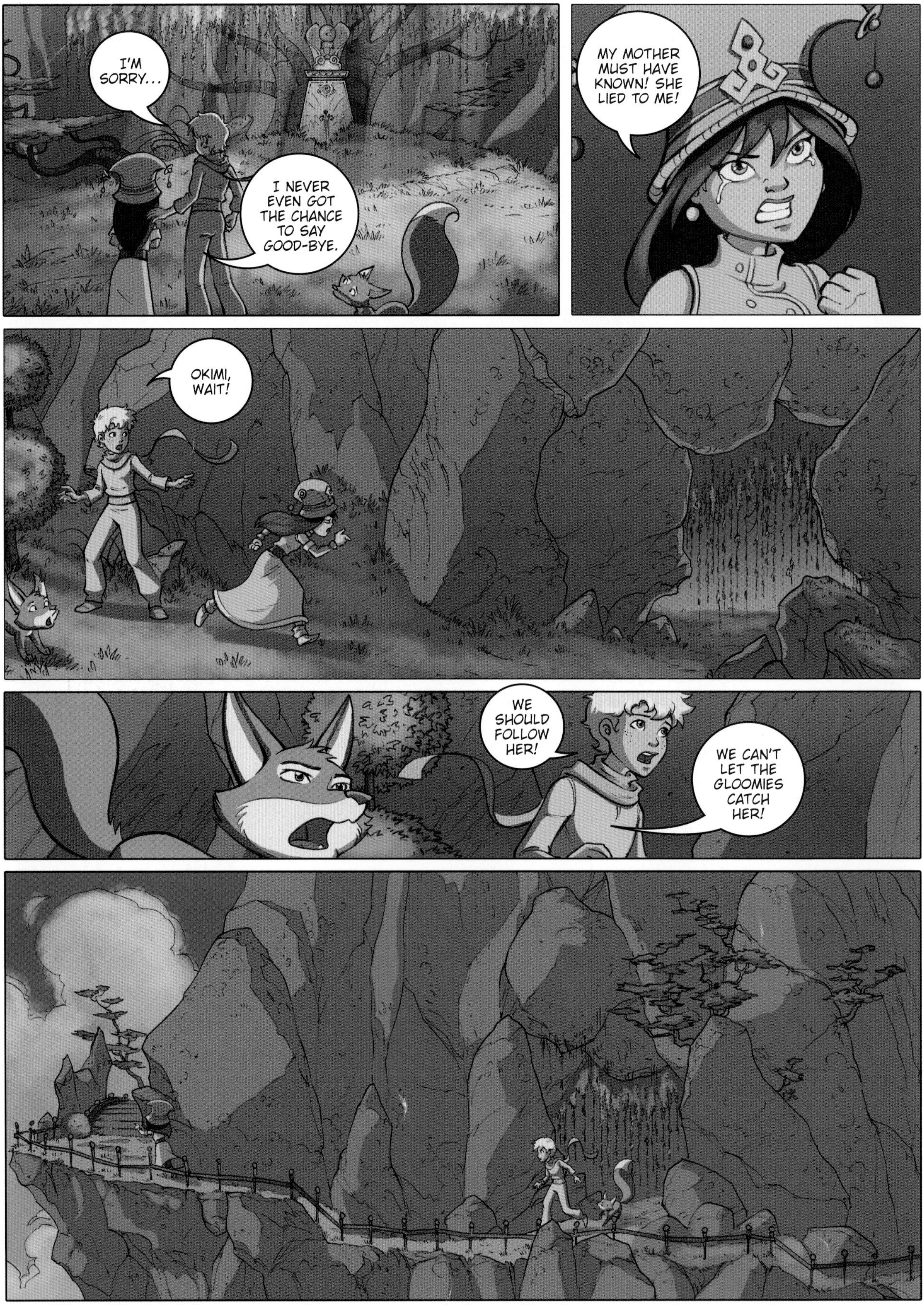
I'M SORRY...
I NEVER EVEN GOT THE CHANCE TO SAY GOOD-BYE.
MY MOTHER MUST HAVE KNOWN! SHE LIED TO ME!
OKIMI, WAIT!
WE SHOULD FOLLOW HER!
WE CAN'T LET THE GLOOMIES CATCH HER!

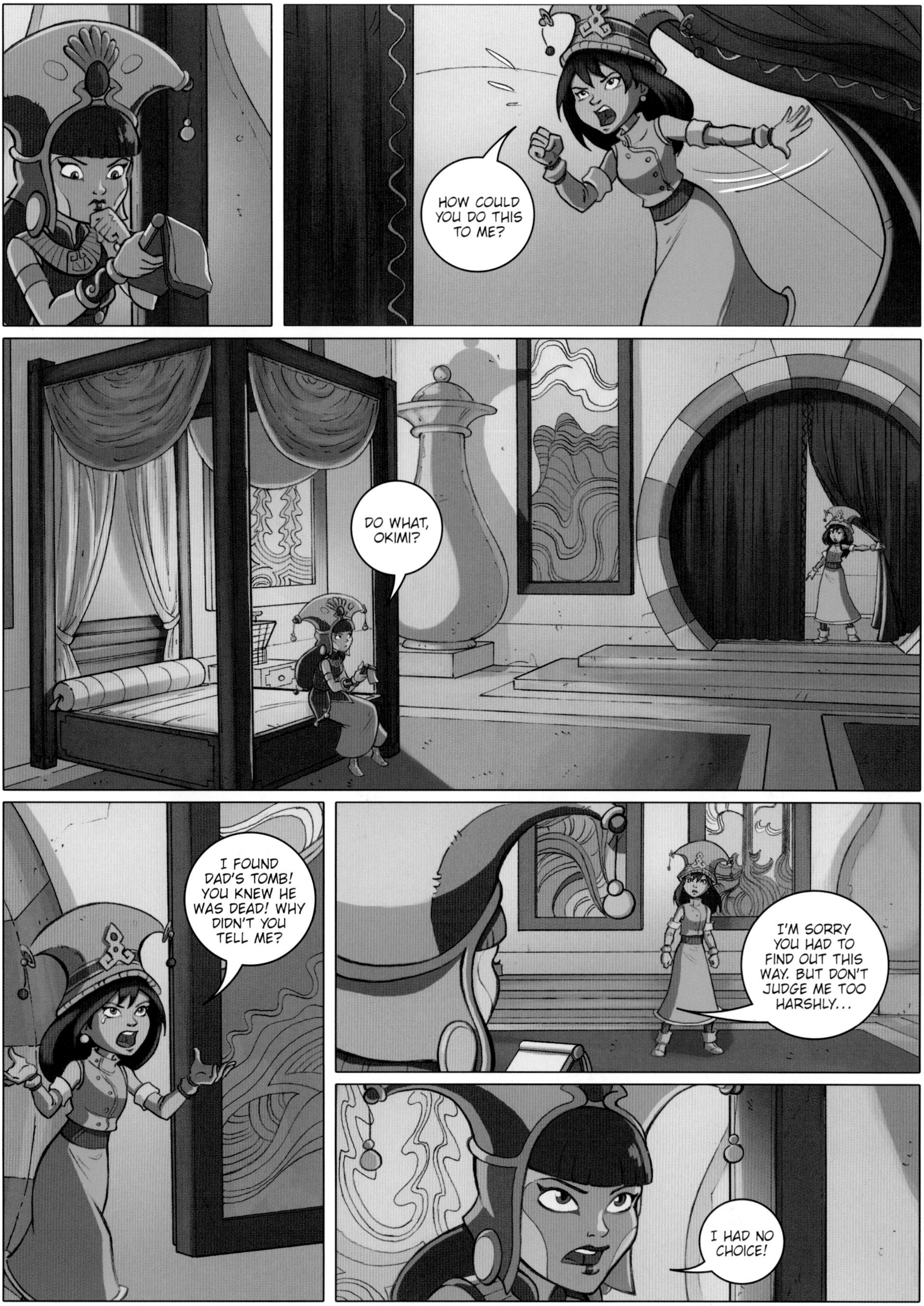
HOW COULD YOU DO THIS TO ME?
DO WHAT, OKIMI?
I FOUND DAD'S TOMB! YOU KNEW HE WAS DEAD! WHY DIDN'T YOU TELL ME?
I'M SORRY YOU HAD TO FIND OUT THIS WAY. BUT DON'T JUDGE ME TOO HARSHLY...
I HAD NO CHOICE!

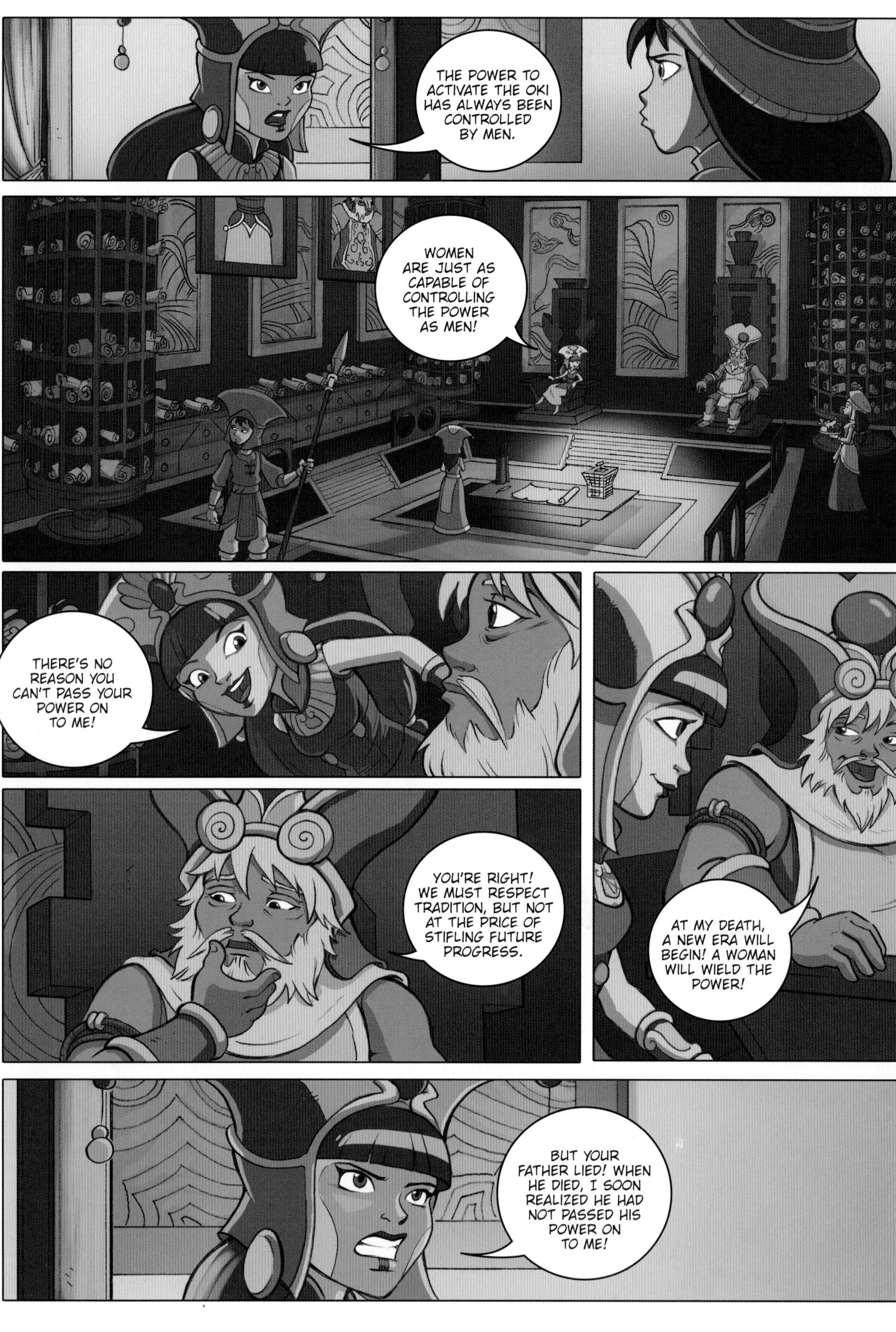
THE POWER TO ACTIVATE THE OKI HAS ALWAYS BEEN CONTROLLED BY MEN.
WOMEN ARE JUST AS CAPABLE OF CONTROLLING THE POWER AS MEN!
THERE'S NO REASON YOU CAN'T PASS YOUR POWER ON TO ME!
YOU'RE RIGHT! WE MUST RESPECT TRADITION, BUT NOT AT THE PRICE OF STIFLING FUTURE PROGRESS.
AT MY DEATH, A NEW ERA WILL BEGIN! A WOMAN WILL WIELD THE POWER!
BUT YOUR FATHER LIED! WHEN HE DIED, I SOON REALIZED HE HAD NOT PASSED HIS POWER ON TO ME!

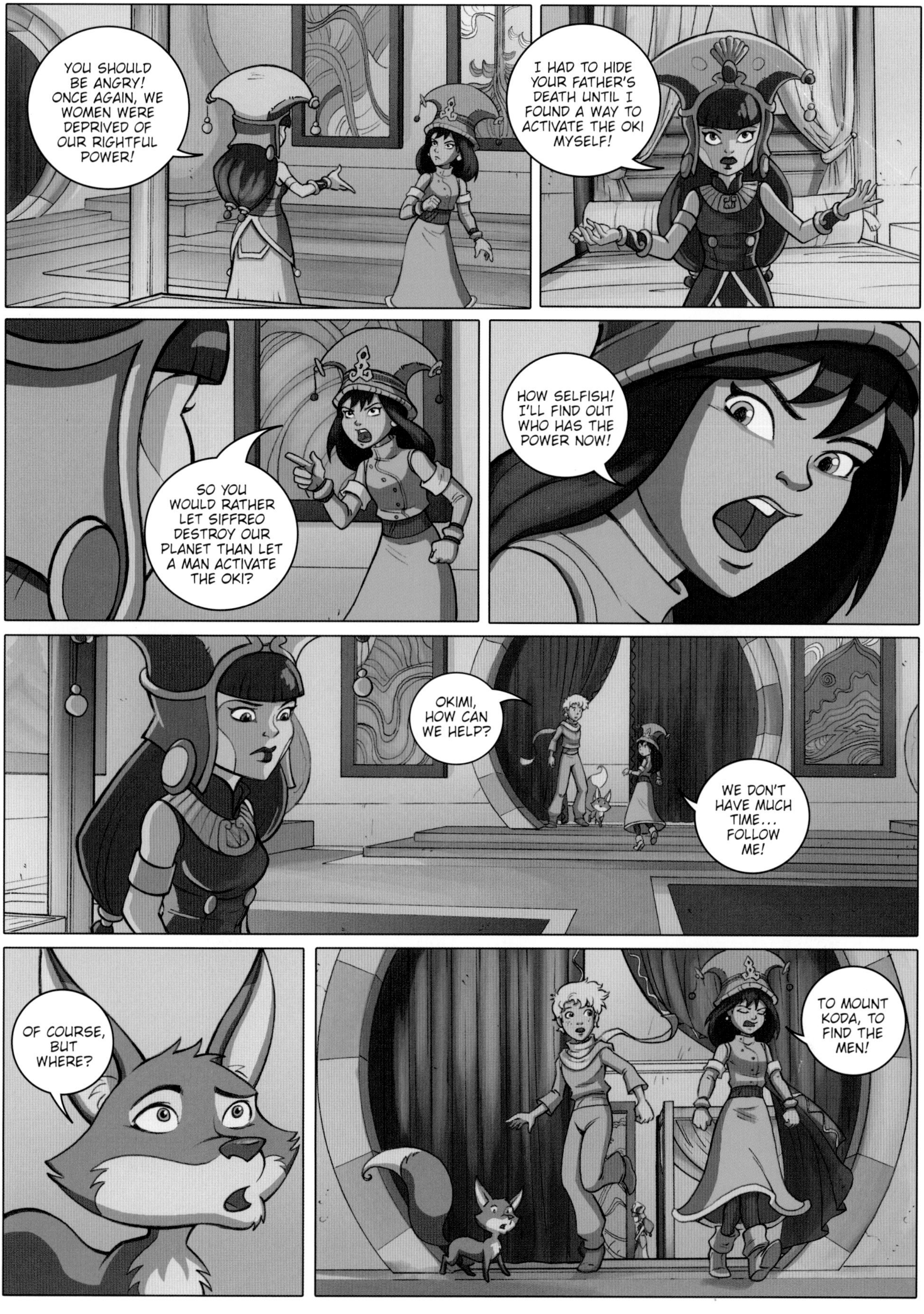
YOU SHOULD BE ANGRY! ONCE AGAIN, WE WOMEN WERE DEPRIVED OF OUR RIGHTFUL POWER!
I HAD TO HIDE YOUR FATHER'S DEATH UNTIL I FOUND A WAY TO ACTIVATE THE OKI MYSELF!
SO YOU WOULD RATHER LET SIFFREO DESTROY OUR PLANET THAN LET A MAN ACTIVATE THE OKI?
HOW SELFISH! I'LL FIND OUT WHO HAS THE POWER NOW!
OKIMI, HOW CAN WE HELP?
WE DON'T HAVE MUCH TIME... FOLLOW ME!
OF COURSE, BUT WHERE?
TO MOUNT KODA, TO FIND THE MEN!

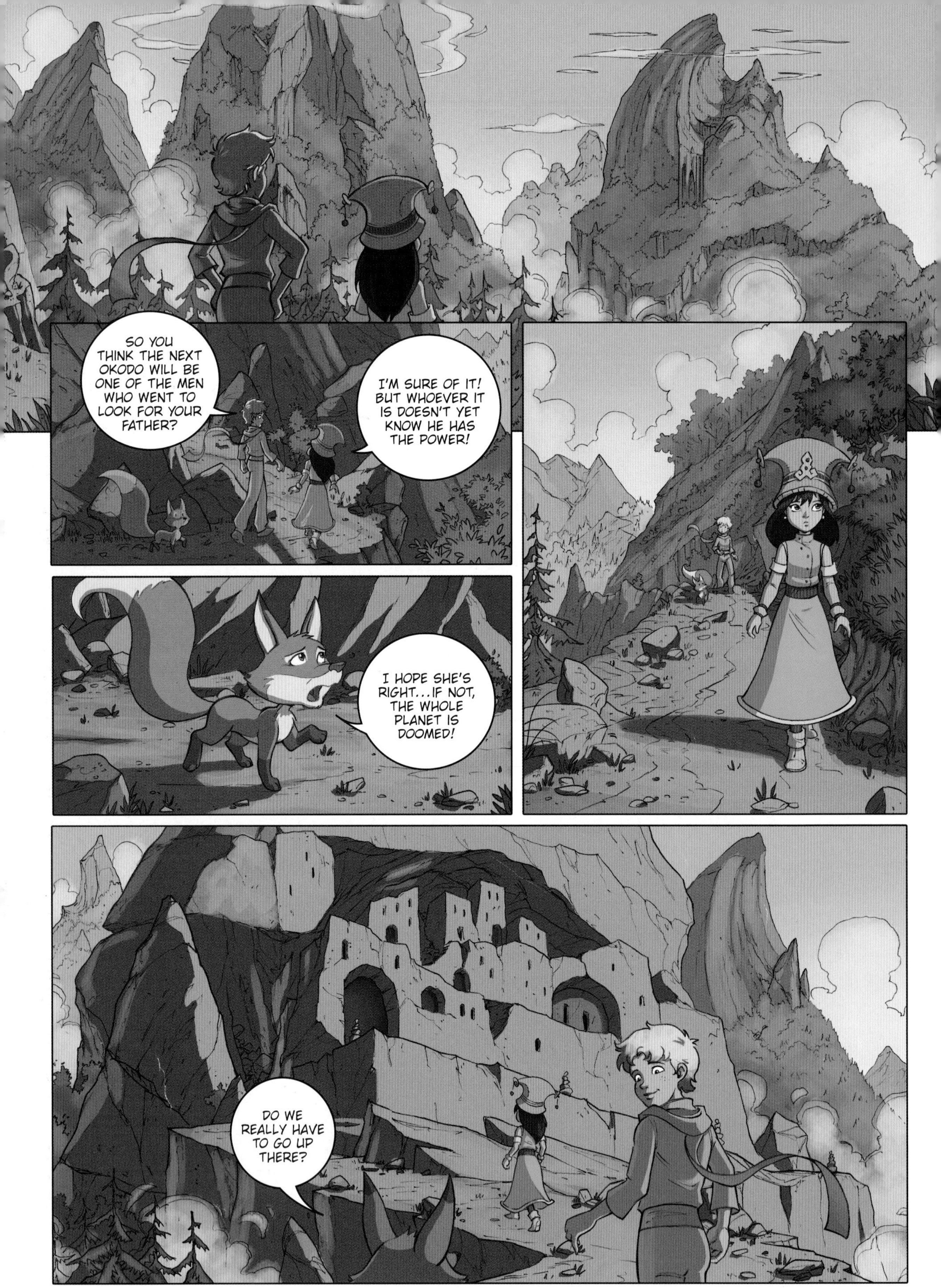

SO YOU THINK THE NEXT OKODO WILL BE ONE OF THE MEN WHO WENT TO LOOK FOR YOUR FATHER?
I'M SURE OF IT! BUT WHOEVER IT IS DOESN'T YET KNOW HE HAS THE POWER!
I HOPE SHE'S RIGHT...IF NOT, THE WHOLE PLANET IS DOOMED!
DO WE REALLY HAVE TO GO UP THERE?

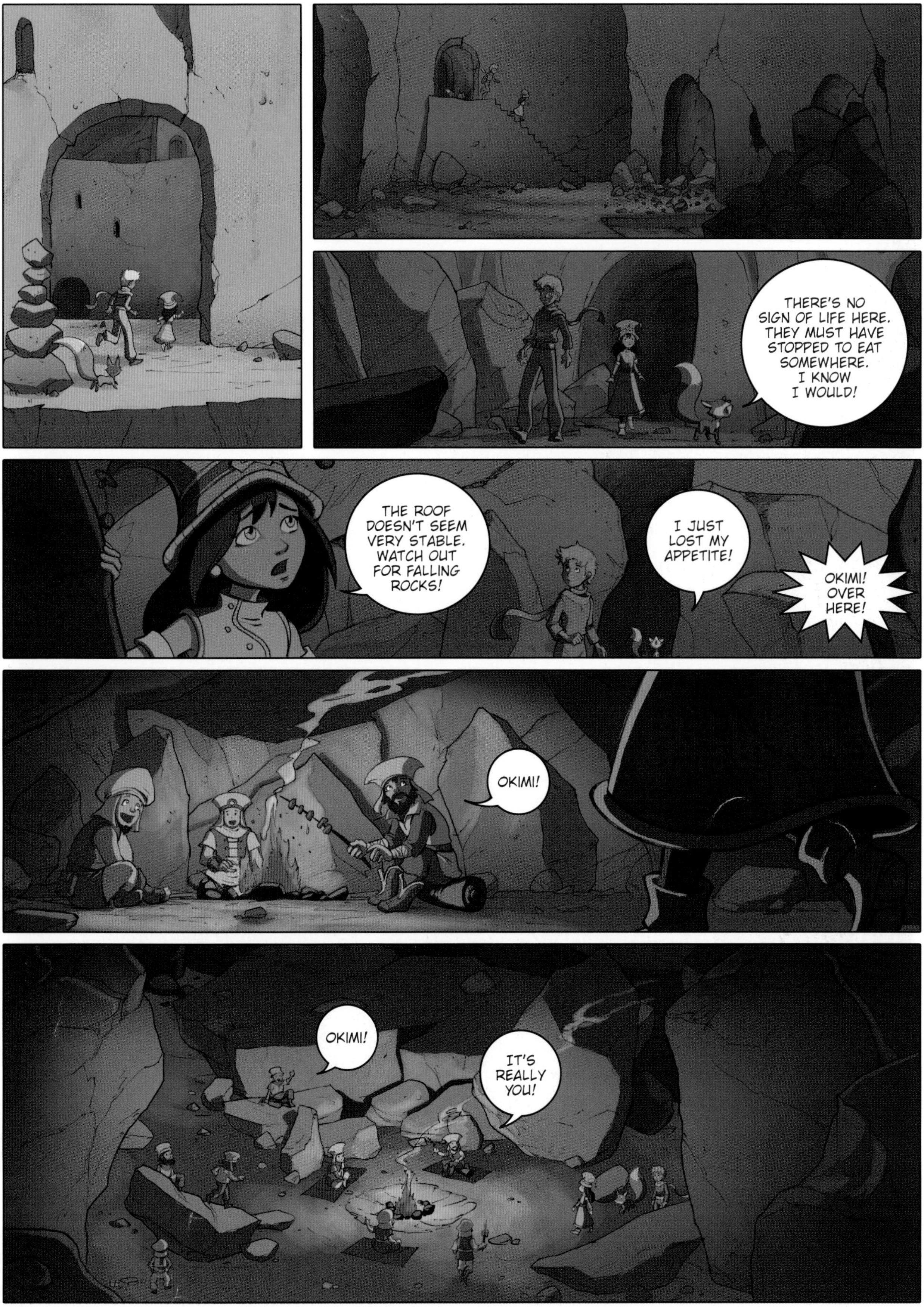
THERE'S NO SIGN OF LIFE HERE. THEY MUST HAVE STOPPED TO EAT SOMEWHERE. I KNOW I WOULD!
THE ROOF DOESN'T SEEM VERY STABLE. WATCH OUT FOR FALLING ROCKS!
I JUST LOST MY APPETITE!
OKIMI! OVER HERE!
OKIMI!
OKIMI!
IT'S REALLY YOU!

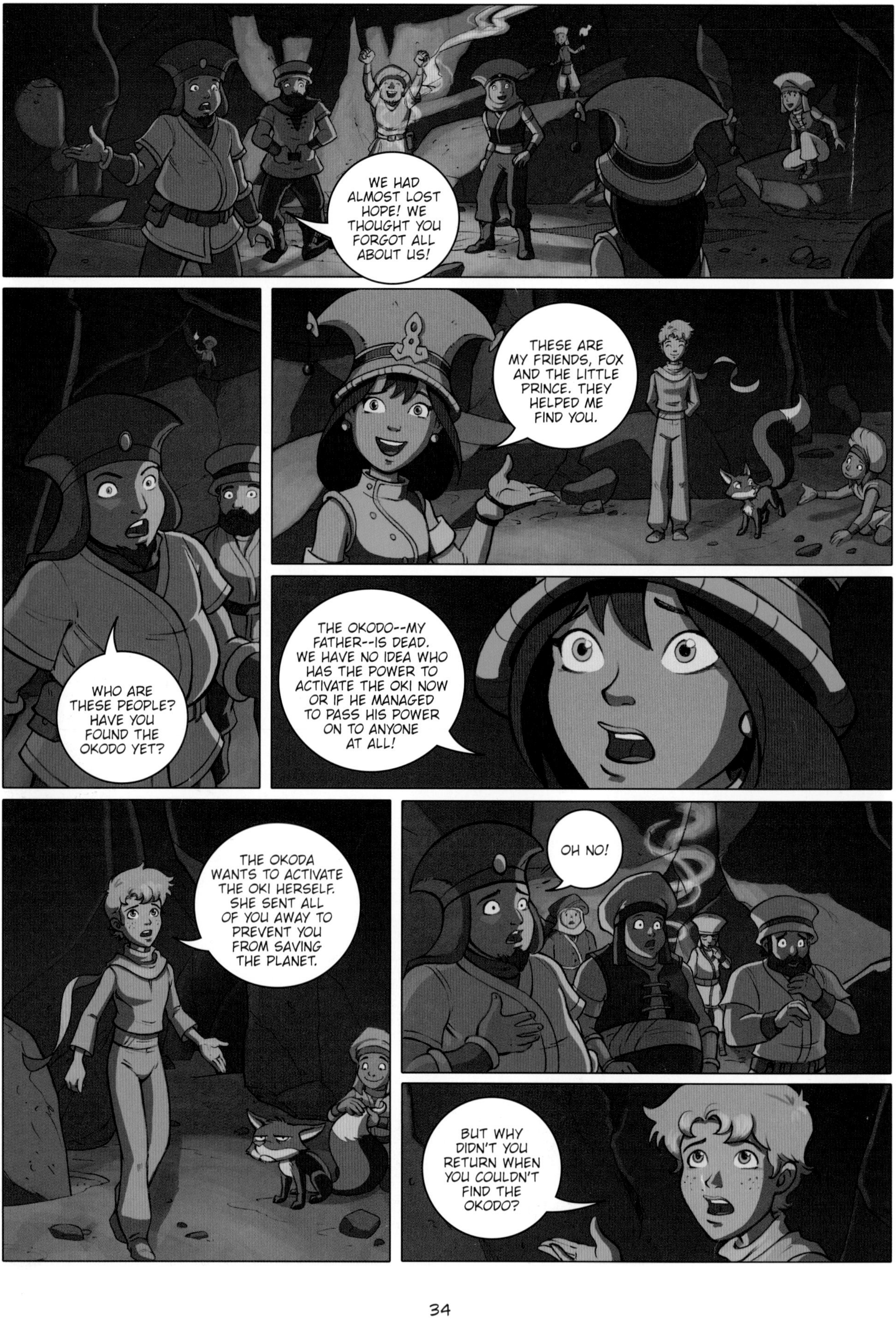
WE HAD ALMOST LOST HOPE! WE THOUGHT YOU FORGOT ALL ABOUT US!
WHO ARE THESE PEOPLE? HAVE YOU FOUND THE OKODO YET?
THESE ARE MY FRIENDS, FOX AND THE LITTLE PRINCE. THEY HELPED ME FIND YOU.
THE OKODO--MY FATHER--IS DEAD. WE HAVE NO IDEA WHO HAS THE POWER TO ACTIVATE THE OKI NOW OR IF HE MANAGED TO PASS HIS POWER ON TO ANYONE AT ALL!
THE OKODA WANTS TO ACTIVATE THE OKI HERSELF. SHE SENT ALL OF YOU AWAY TO PREVENT YOU FROM SAVING THE PLANET.
OH NO!
BUT WHY DIDN'T YOU RETURN WHEN YOU COULDN'T FIND THE OKODO?

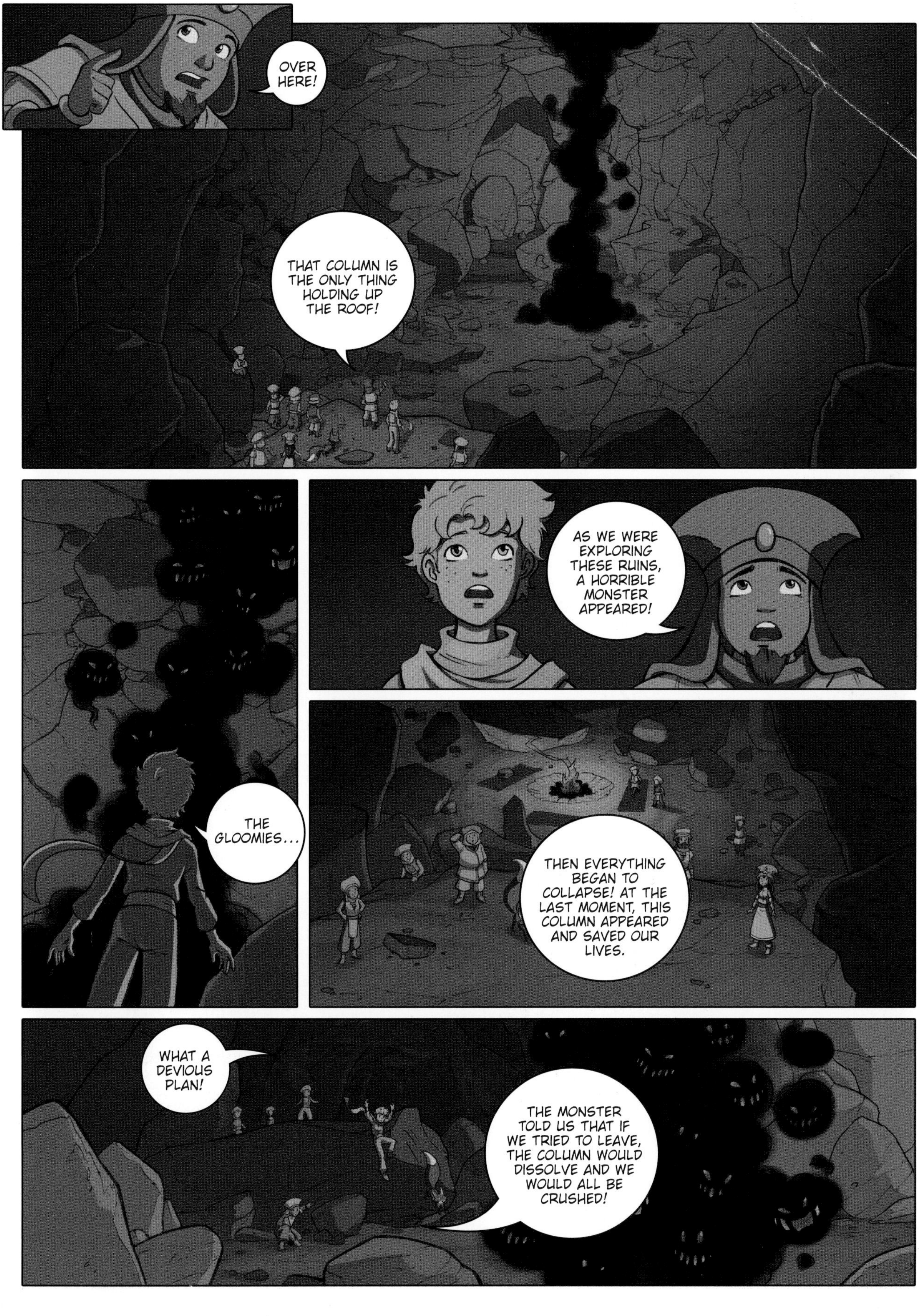
OVER HERE!
THAT COLUMN IS THE ONLY THING HOLDING UP THE ROOF!
THE GLOOMIES...
AS WE WERE EXPLORING THESE RUINS, A HORRIBLE MONSTER APPEARED!
THEN EVERYTHING BEGAN TO COLLAPSE! AT THE LAST MOMENT, THIS COLUMN APPEARED AND SAVED OUR LIVES.
WHAT A DEVIOUS PLAN!
THE MONSTER TOLD US THAT IF WE TRIED TO LEAVE, THE COLUMN WOULD DISSOLVE AND WE WOULD ALL BE CRUSHED!

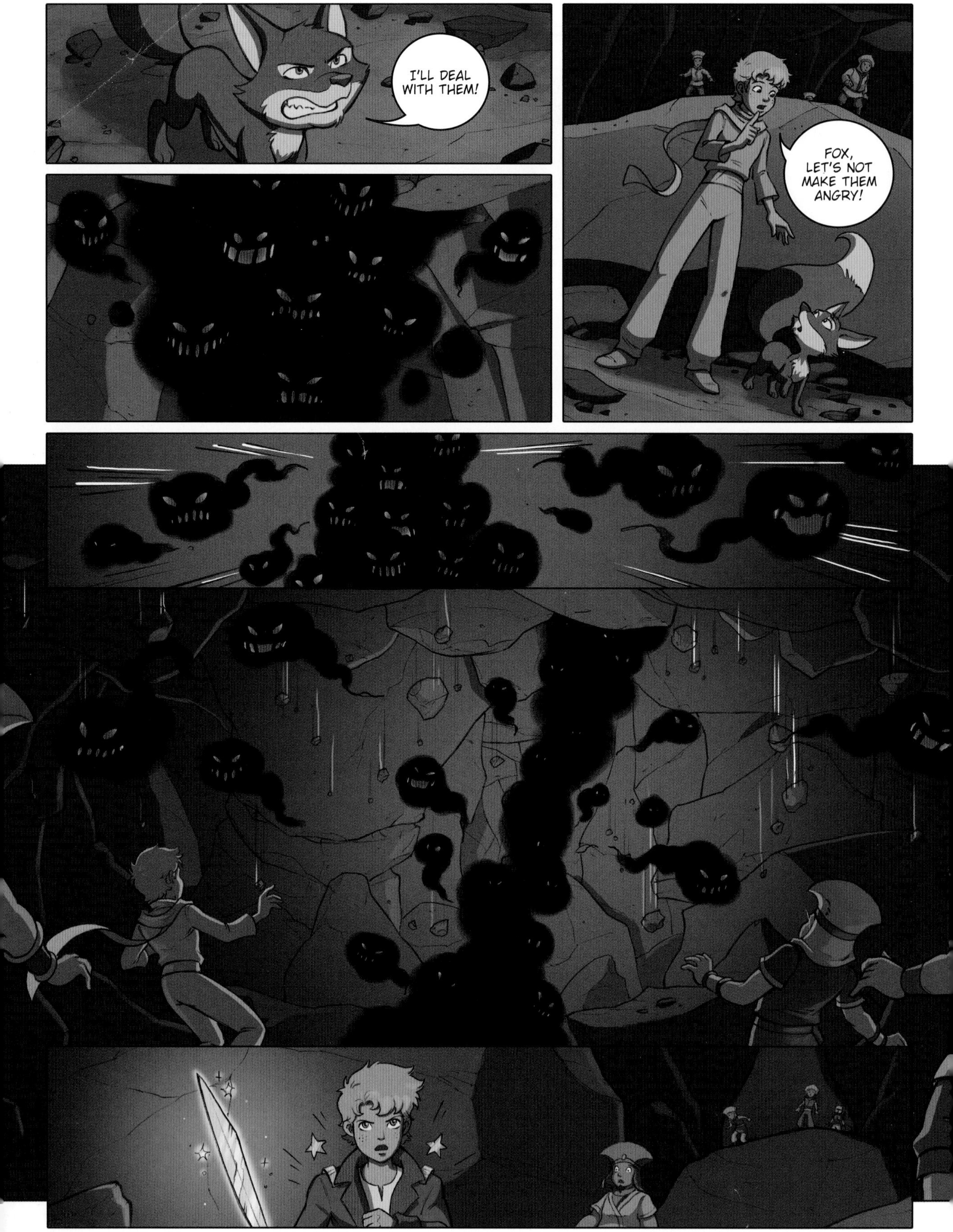
I'LL DEAL WITH THEM!
FOX, LET'S NOT MAKE THEM ANGRY!

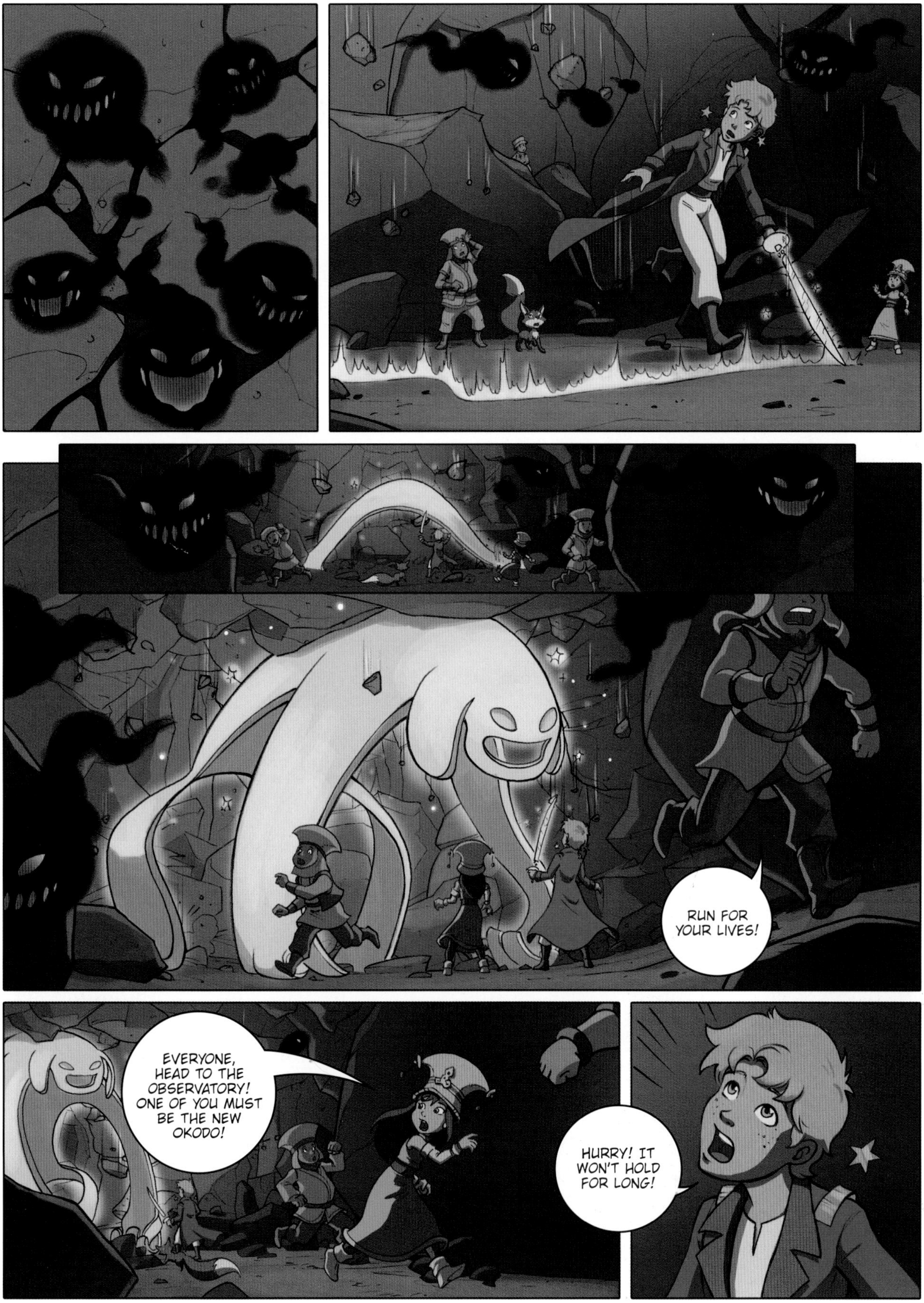
RUN FOR YOUR LIVES!
EVERYONE, HEAD TO THE OBSERVATORY! ONE OF YOU MUST BE THE NEW OKODO!
HURRY! IT WON'T HOLD FOR LONG!

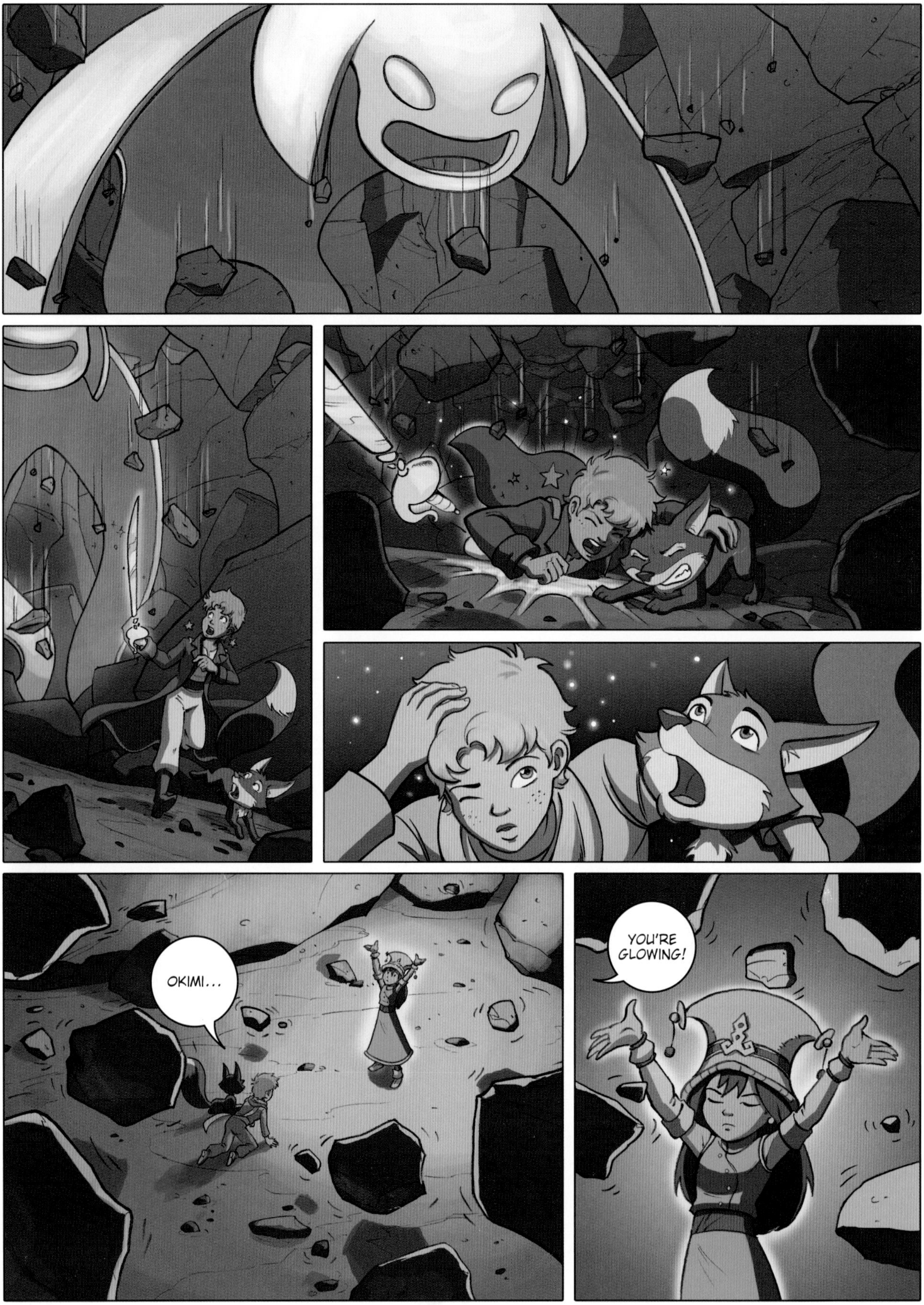
OKIMI...
YOU'RE GLOWING!

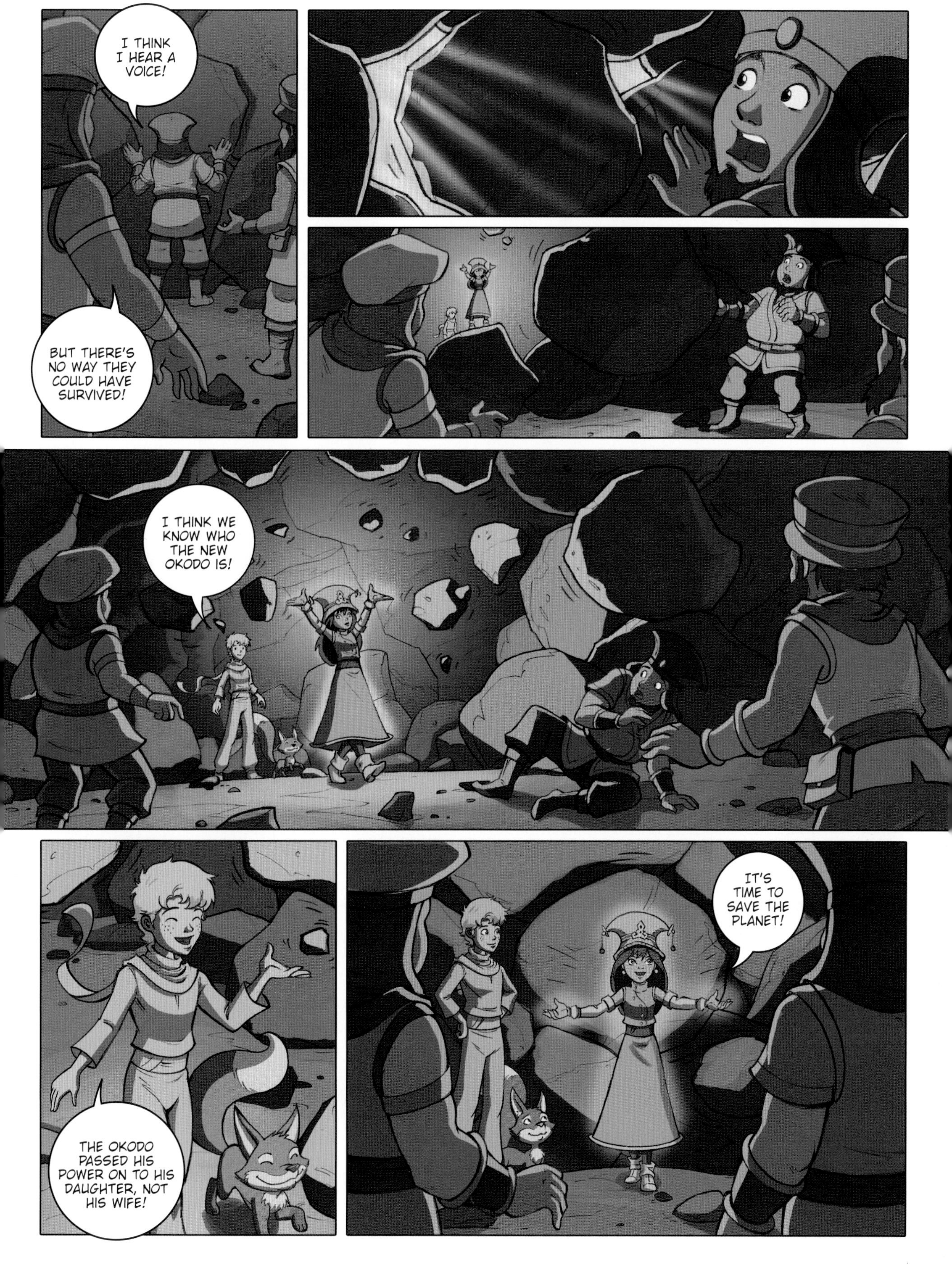
I THINK I HEAR A VOICE!
BUT THERE'S NO WAY THEY COULD HAVE SURVIVED!
I THINK WE KNOW WHO THE NEW OKODO IS!
THE OKODO PASSED HIS POWER ON TO HIS DAUGHTER, NOT HIS WIFE!
IT'S TIME TO SAVE THE PLANET!

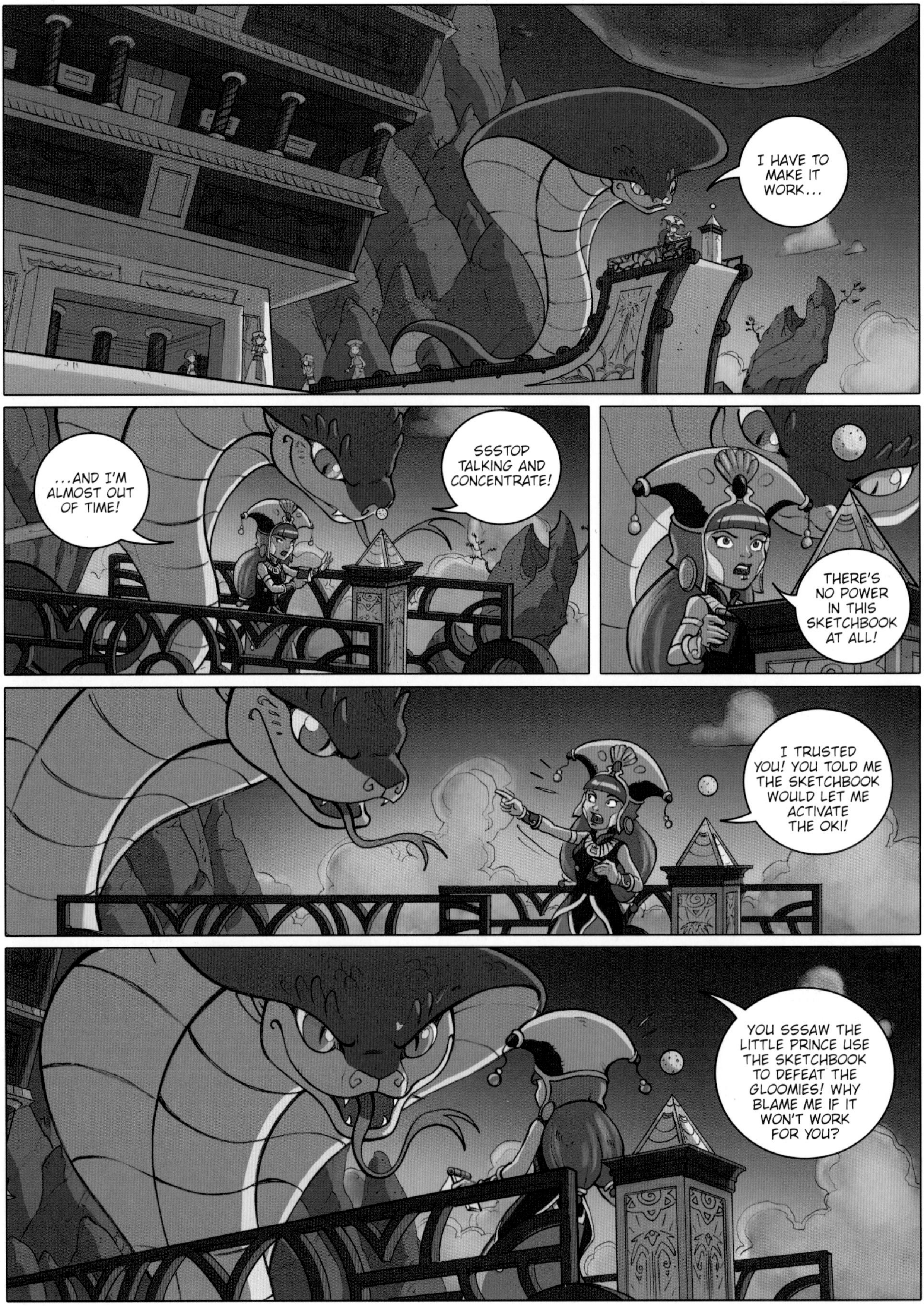

I HAVE TO MAKE IT WORK...
...AND I'M ALMOST OUT OF TIME!
SSSTOP TALKING AND CONCENTRATE!
THERE'S NO POWER IN THIS SKETCHBOOK AT ALL!
I TRUSTED YOU! YOU TOLD ME THE SKETCHBOOK WOULD LET ME ACTIVATE THE OKI!
YOU SSSAW THE LITTLE PRINCE USE THE SKETCHBOOK TO DEFEAT THE GLOOMIES! WHY BLAME ME IF IT WON'T WORK FOR YOU?

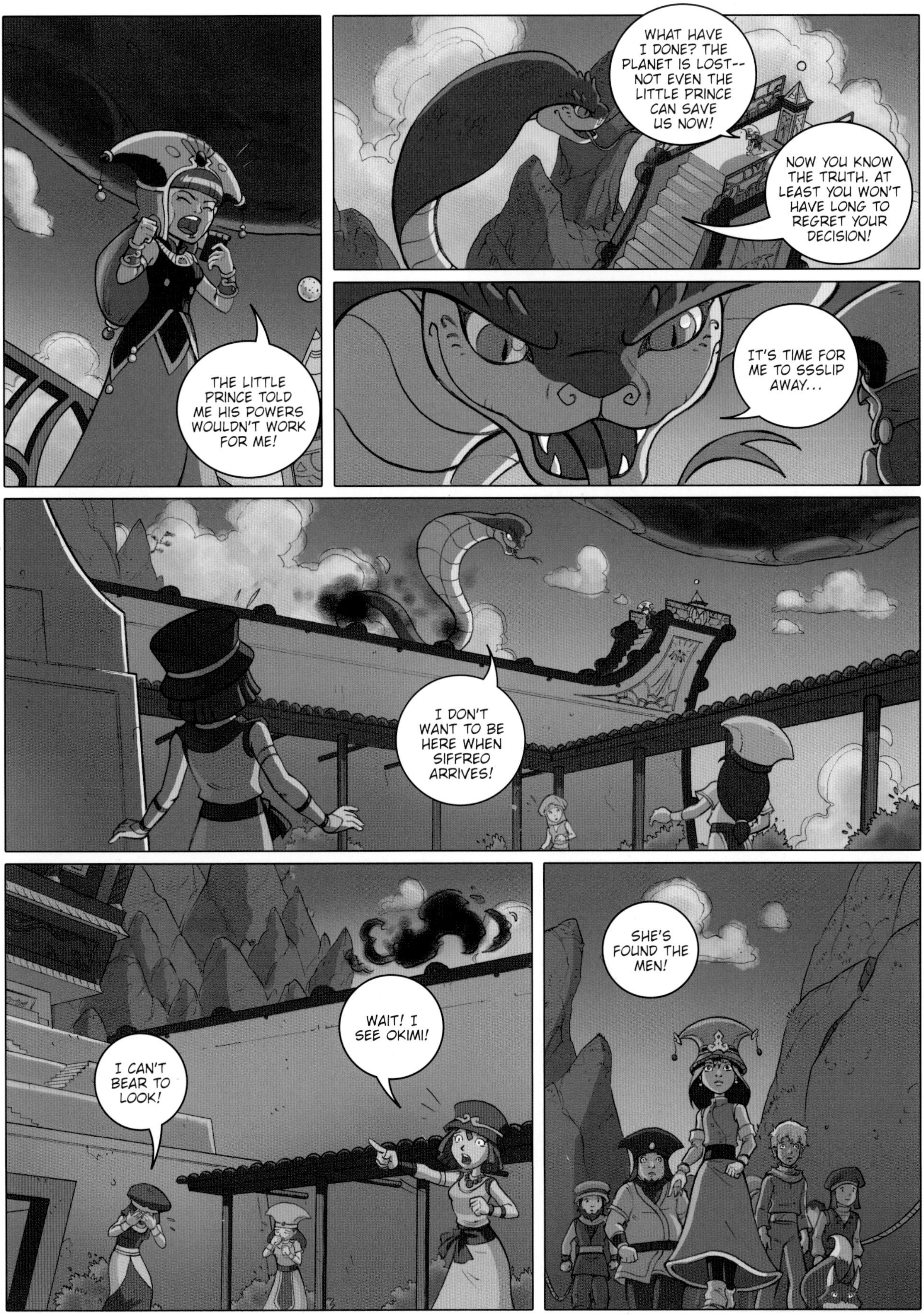
THE LITTLE PRINCE TOLD ME HIS POWERS WOULDN'T WORK FOR ME!
WHAT HAVE I DONE? THE PLANET IS LOST-- NOT EVEN THE LITTLE PRINCE CAN SAVE US NOW!
NOW YOU KNOW THE TRUTH. AT LEAST YOU WON'T HAVE LONG TO REGRET YOUR DECISION!
IT'S TIME FOR ME TO SSSLIP AWAY...
I DON'T WANT TO BE HERE WHEN SIFFREO ARRIVES!
I CAN'T BEAR TO LOOK!
WAIT! I SEE OKIMI!
SHE'S FOUND THE MEN!

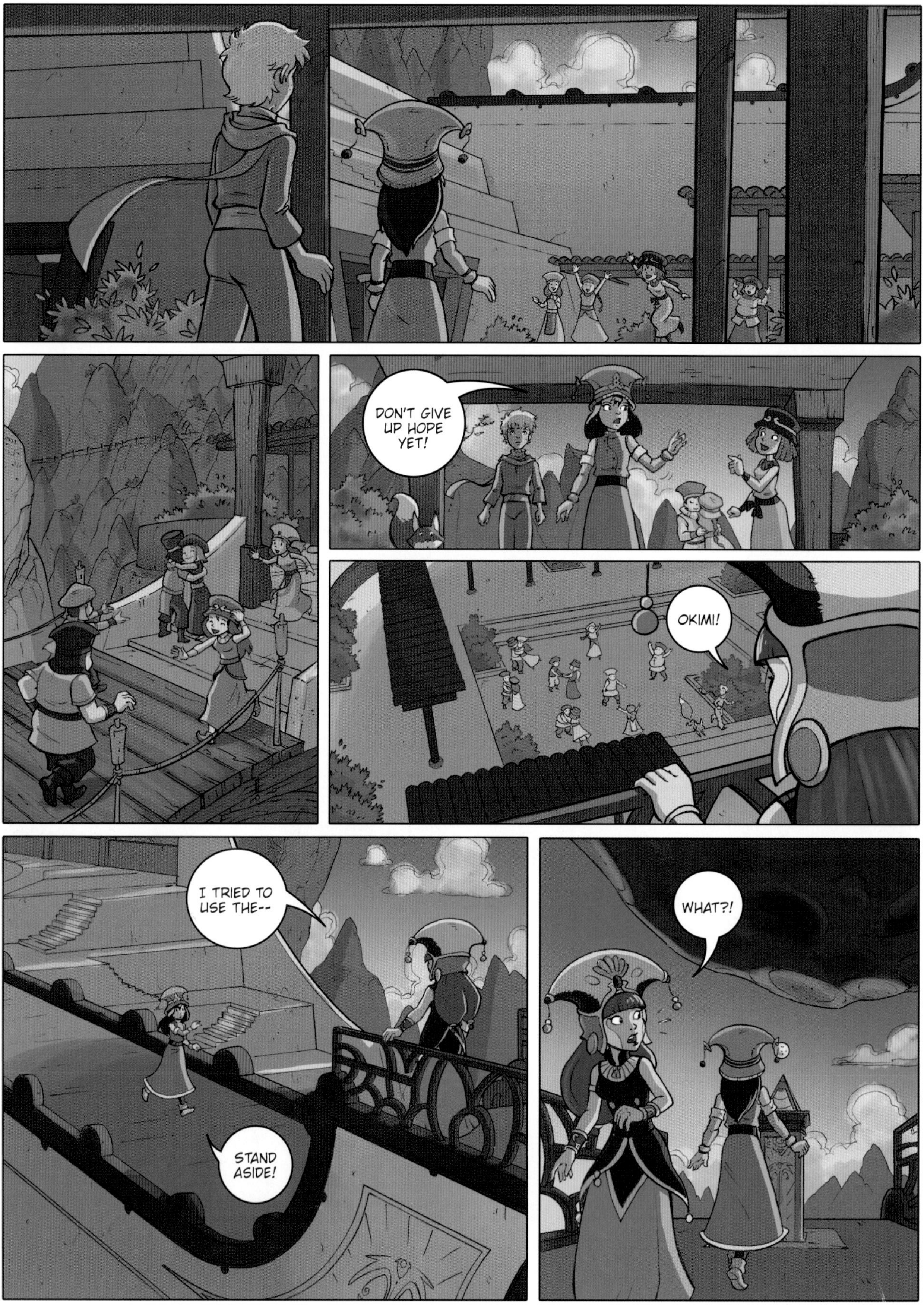
DON'T GIVE UP HOPE YET!
OKIMI!
I TRIED TO USE THE--
STAND ASIDE!
WHAT?!

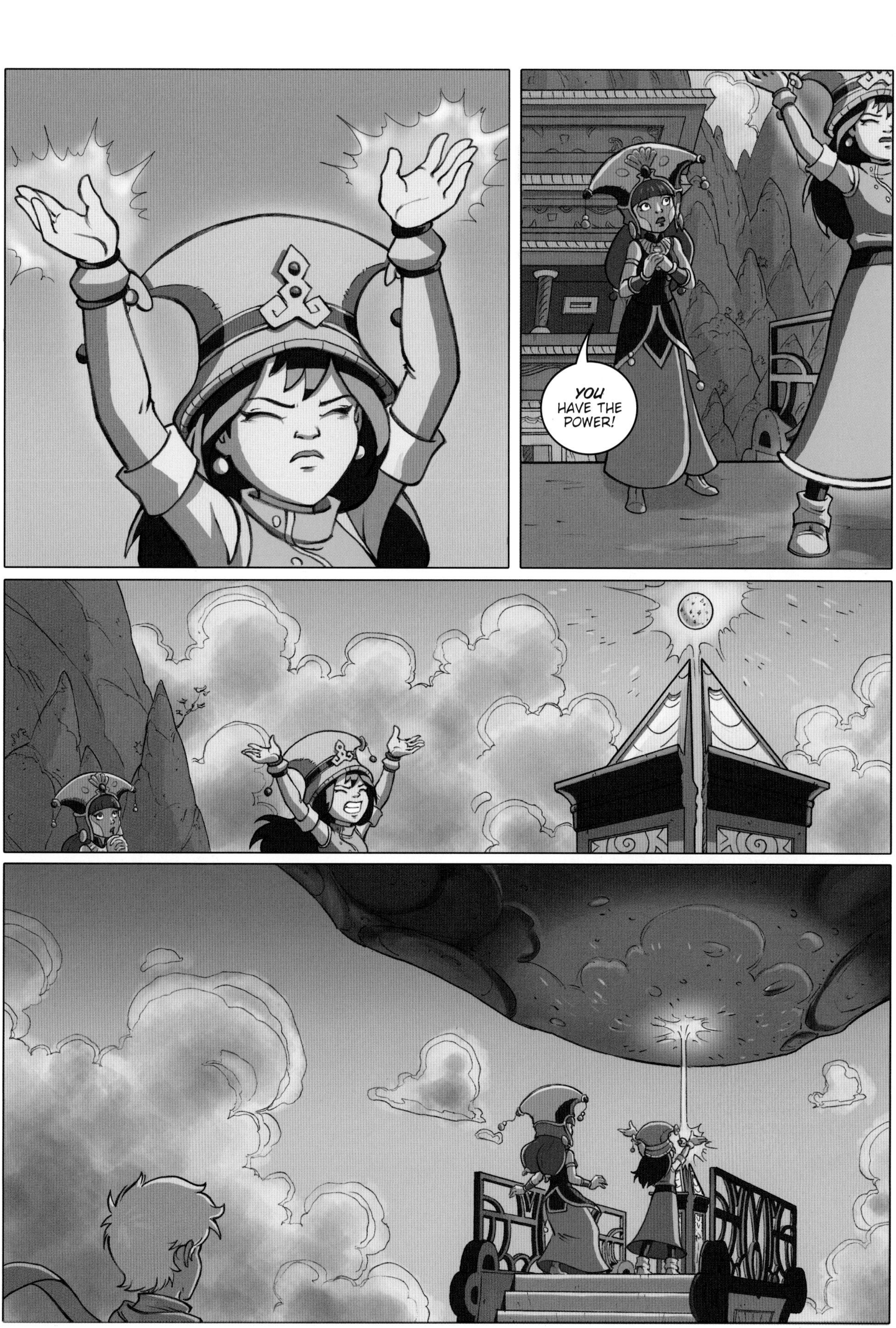
YOU HAVE THE POWER!

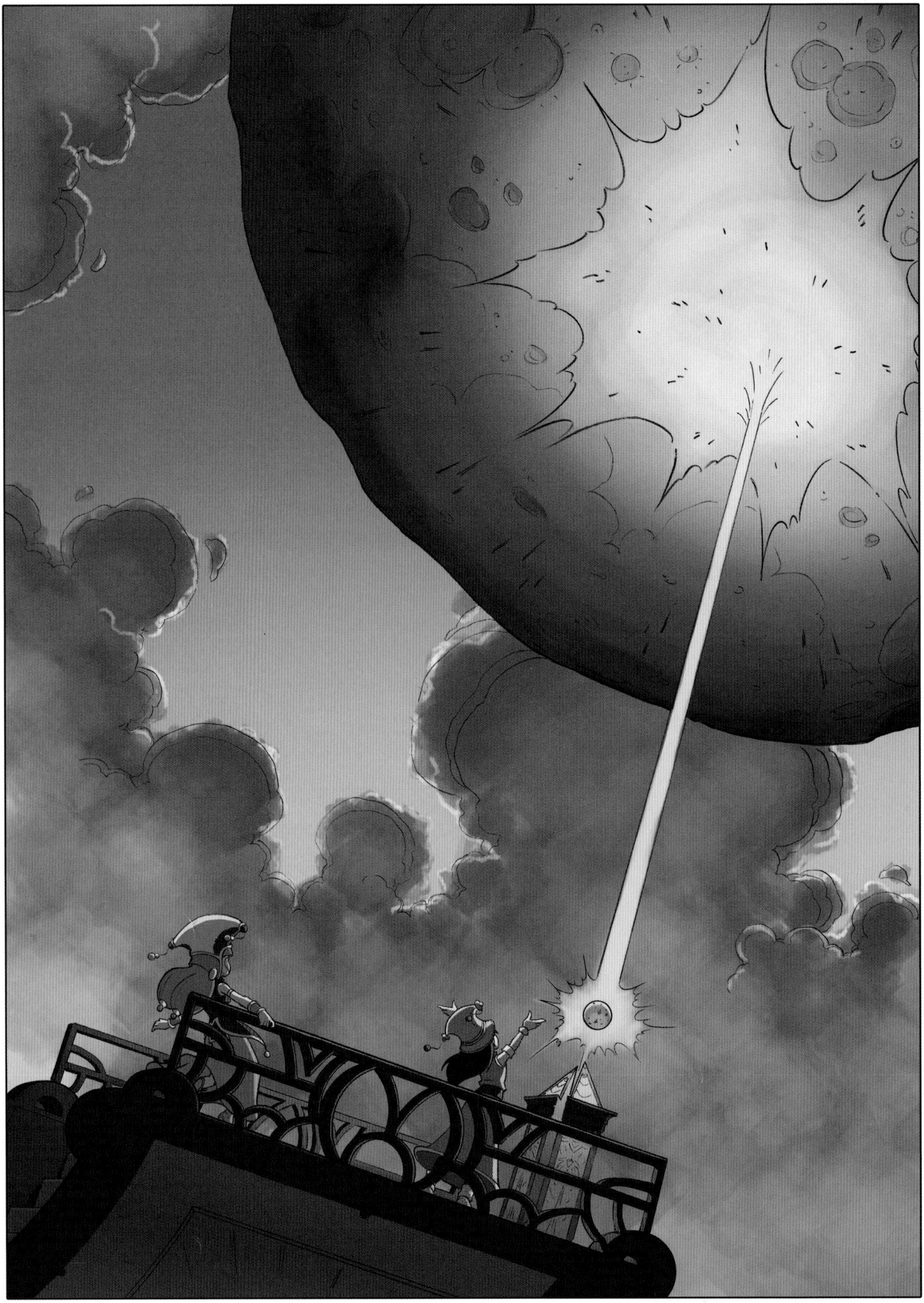

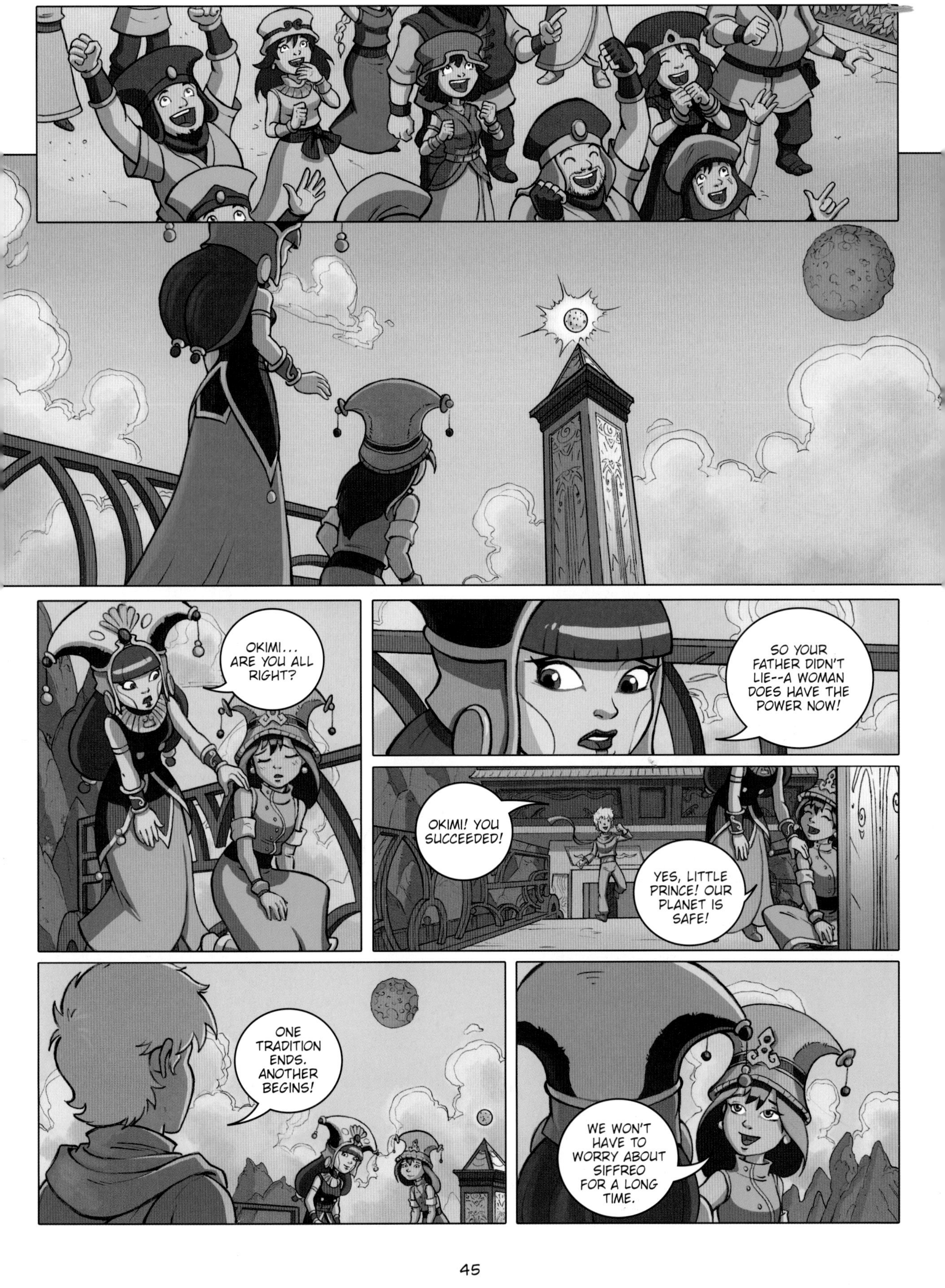
OKIMI... ARE YOU ALL RIGHT?
SO YOUR FATHER DIDN'T LIE--A WOMAN DOES HAVE THE POWER NOW!
OKIMI! YOU SUCCEEDED!
YES, LITTLE PRINCE! OUR PLANET IS SAFE!
ONE TRADITION ENDS. ANOTHER BEGINS!
WE WON'T HAVE TO WORRY ABOUT SIFFREO FOR A LONG TIME.

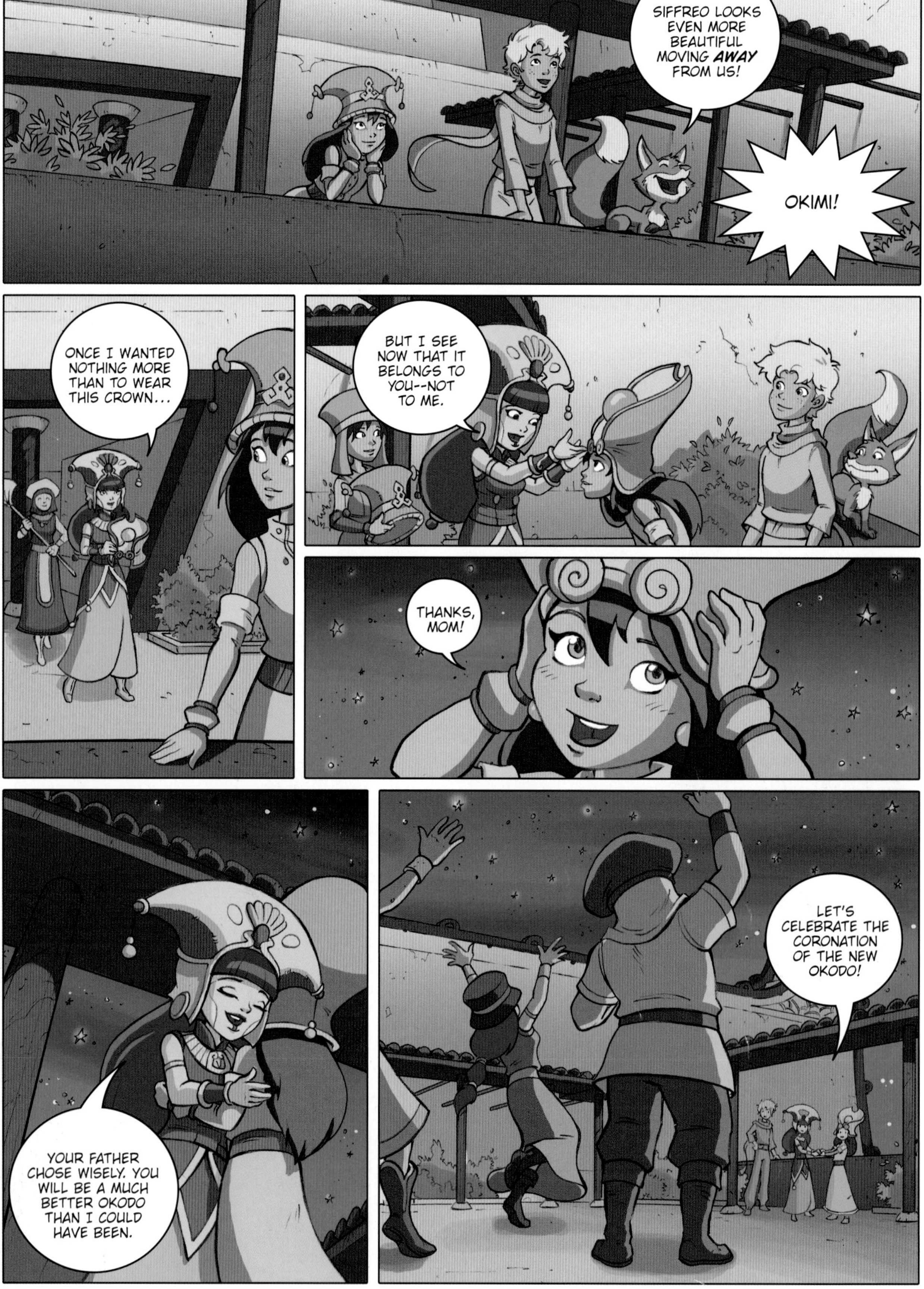
SIFFREO LOOKS EVEN MORE BEAUTIFUL MOVING AWAY FROM US!
OKIMI!
ONCE I WANTED NOTHING MORE THAN TO WEAR THIS CROWN...
BUT I SEE NOW THAT IT BELONGS TO YOU--NOT TO ME.
THANKS, MOM!
YOUR FATHER CHOSE WISELY. YOU WILL BE A MUCH BETTER OKODO THAN I COULD HAVE BEEN.
LET'S CELEBRATE THE CORONATION OF THE NEW OKODO!

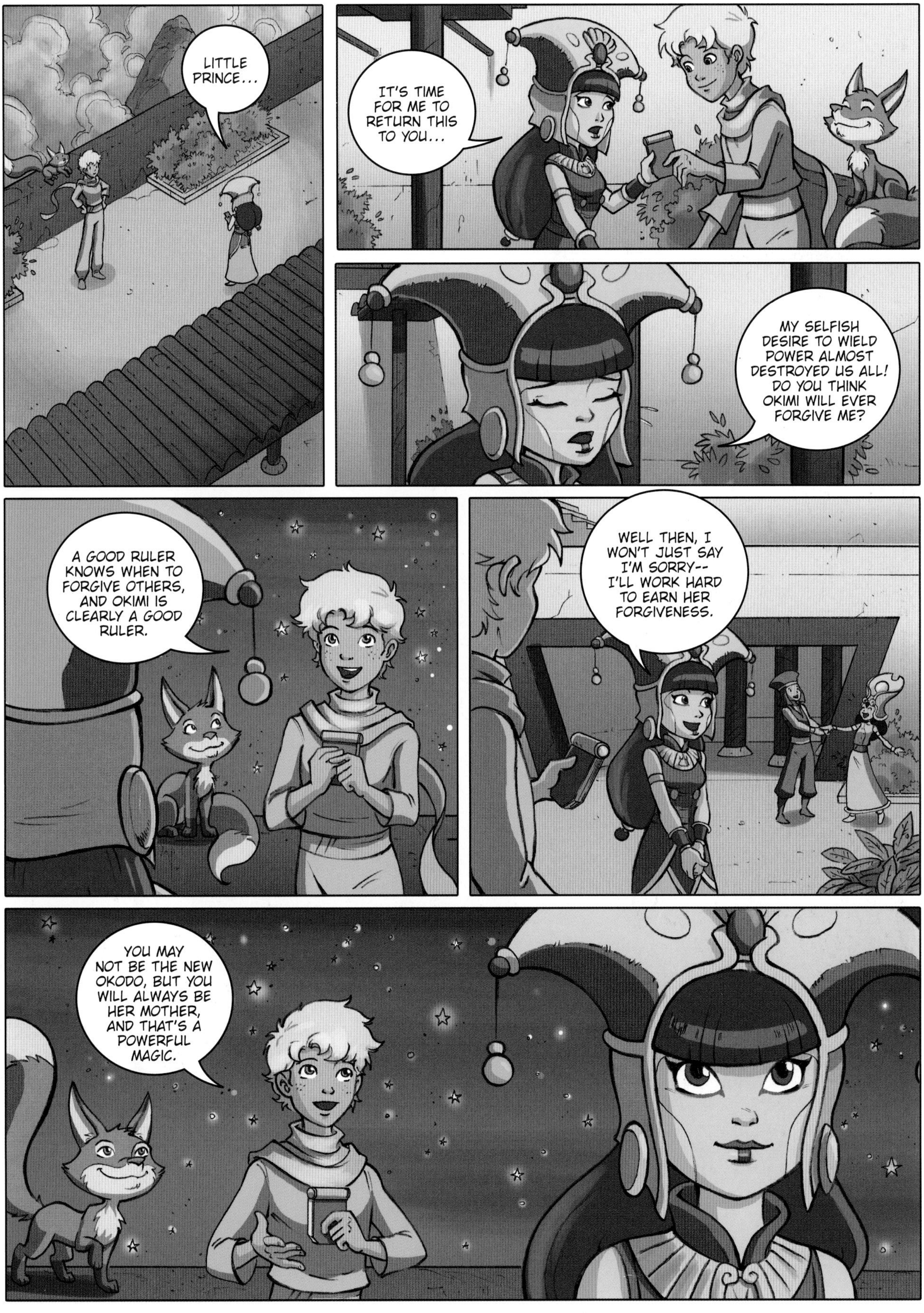
LITTLE PRINCE...
IT'S TIME FOR ME TO RETURN THIS TO YOU...
MY SELFISH DESIRE TO WIELD POWER ALMOST DESTROYED US ALL! DO YOU THINK OKIMI WILL EVER FORGIVE ME?
A GOOD RULER KNOWS WHEN TO FORGIVE OTHERS, AND OKIMI IS CLEARLY A GOOD RULER.
WELL THEN, I WON'T JUST SAY I'M SORRY-- I'LL WORK HARD TO EARN HER FORGIVENESS.
YOU MAY NOT BE THE NEW OKODO, BUT YOU WILL ALWAYS BE HER MOTHER, AND THAT'S A POWERFUL MAGIC.

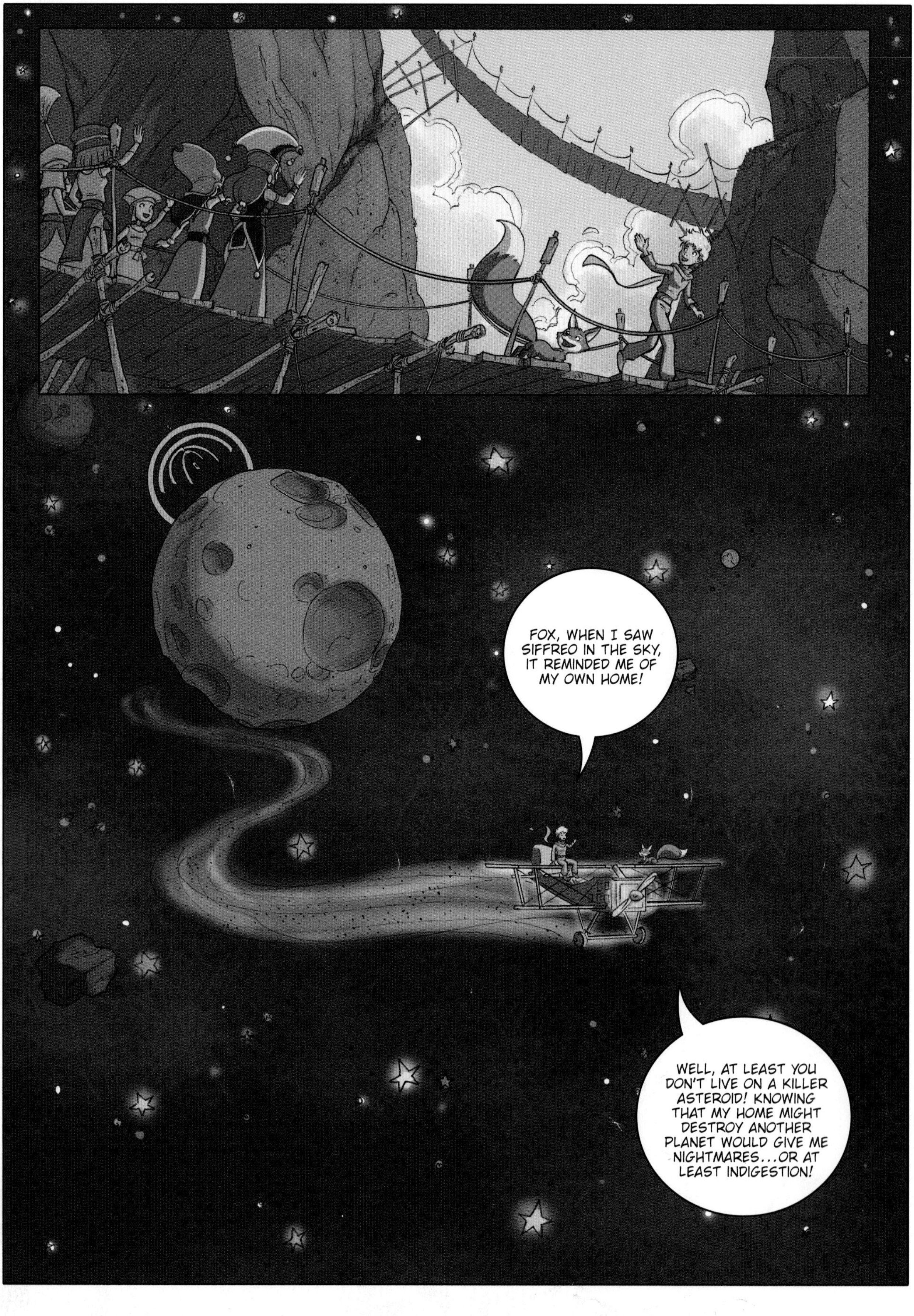
FOX, WHEN I SAW SIFFREO IN THE SKY, IT REMINDED ME OF MY OWN HOME!
WELL, AT LEAST YOU DON'T LIVE ON A KILLER ASTEROID! KNOWING THAT MY HOME MIGHT DESTROY ANOTHER PLANET WOULD GIVE ME NIGHTMARES...OR AT LEAST INDIGESTION!

Read all the Books in *The Little Prince* series

Book 1: The Planet of Wind

Book 2: The Planet of the Firebird

Book 3: The Planet of Music

Book 4: The Planet of Jade

Book 5: The Star Snatcher's Planet

Book 6: The Planet of the Night Globes

Book 7: The Planet of the Overhearers

Book 8: The Planet of the Tortoise Driver

Book 9 : The Planet of the Giant

Book 10 : The Planet of Trainiacs

Book 11 : The Planet of Libris

Book 12 : The Planet of Ludokaa

Book 13 : The Planet of Tear-Eaters

Book 14 : The Planet of the Grand Buffoon

Book 15 : The Planet of the Gargand

Book 16 : The Planet of Gehom

Book 17 : The Planet of the Bubble Gob

Book 18 : The Planet of Time

Book 19 : The Planet of the Cublix

Book 20 : The Planet of Coppelius

Book 21 : The Planet of Okidians

Book 22 : The Planet of Ashkabaar

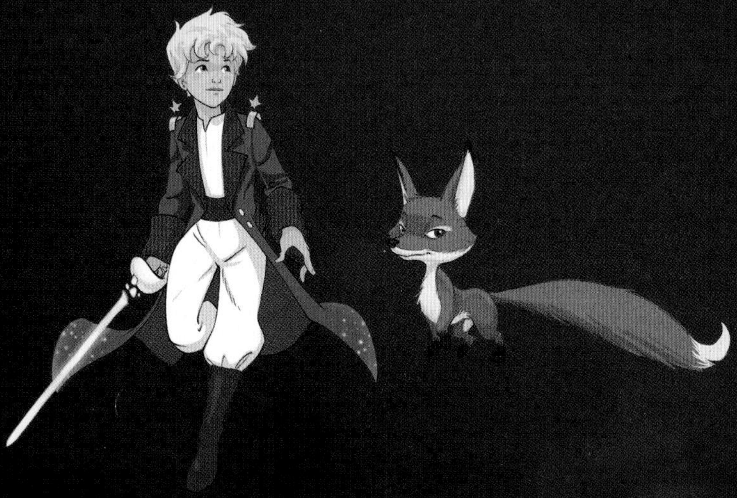

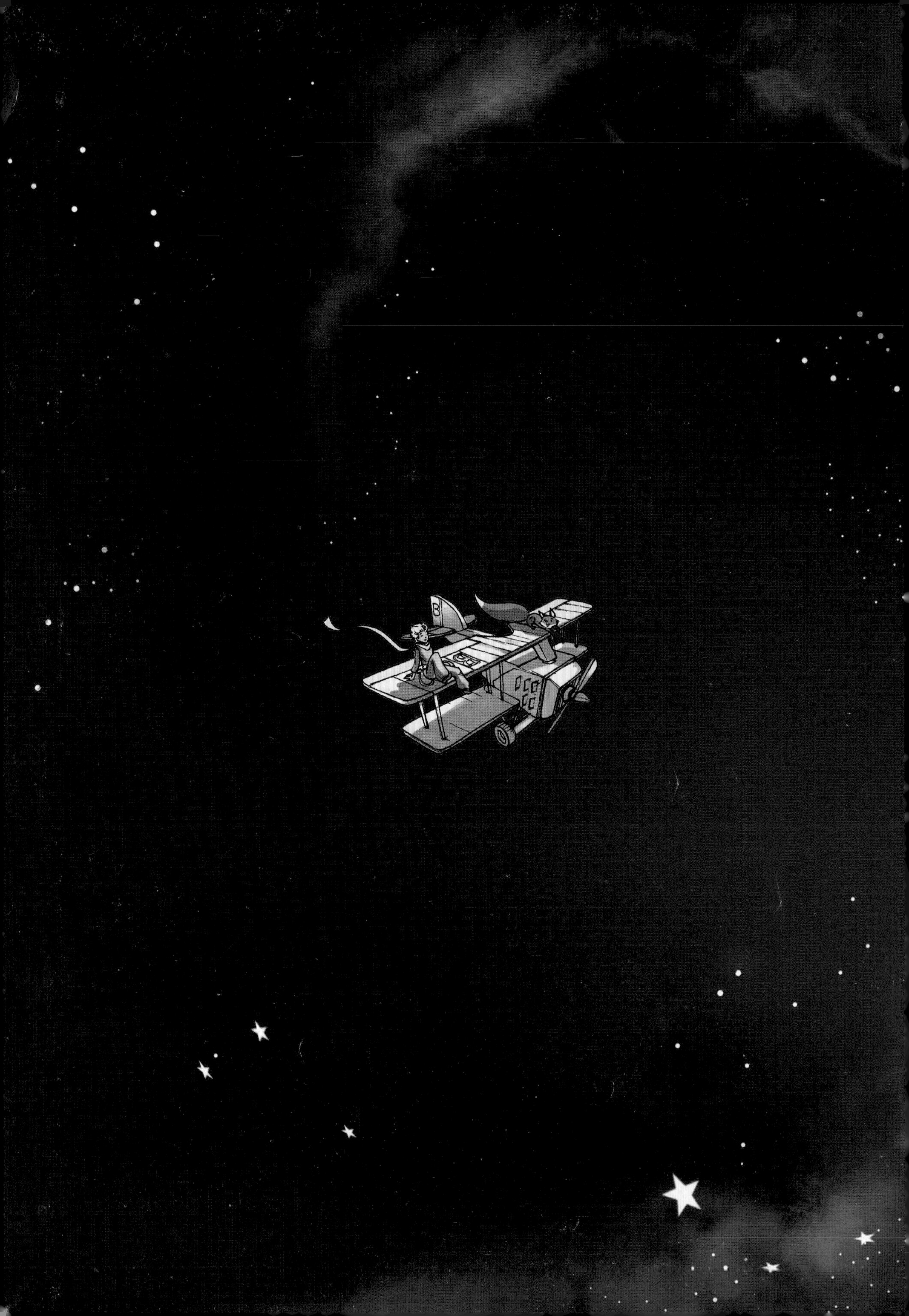